Mistress Christmas

...all signs point North for not-so-Saint-Nick

In a rare moment of recklessness, mild-mannered accountant Holly North lets her best friend guilt her into filling in as Mistress Christmas at Sugar Plums, a Christmas-themed strip club. Fearing she'll be recognized—or worse, considered a fraud—she dons a velvet mask along with the Mrs. Claus-meets-dominatrix costume. She's shocked at how deliciously wicked anonymity feels.

Detective Nick West is determined to discover how his friend was supposedly robbed after a lap dance at Sugar Plums. His visions of revenge vanish faster than a flying sleigh upon his first peek at Mistress Christmas—a leggy brunette with smoky eyes and a lush mouth begging for hours beneath the mistletoe.

Their attraction flares hotter than a fireplace on a cold winter evening, and Nick is only too happy to oblige when Holly blurts out her one Christmas wish...

For a naughty secret Santa to sweep her away for a night of anonymous sexual pleasure.

Warning: This erotic comedy contains naughty holiday innuendo, creative use of garland, sexy love scenes hot as spiced cider, a heroine as sweet as sugared plums, and a wildly romantic hero with a great big...candy cane.

Miss Firecracker

She's the match, he's the fuse...an explosive combination

One year ago Willow Gregory entered the Miss Firecracker contest on a dare—and ended up with the crown. As a working carpenter, she's not exactly the tears-and-tiara type, and after a year of walking the straight and narrow she's ready to cut loose.

Waking up in a sexy stranger's bed with no memory of the havoc she wreaked the night before wasn't quite what she had in mind. Nor was agreeing to his mandate—work for him at the tavern until she repays the damage. Or go to jail.

Blake West thinks he could possibly be the only man alive who could say no to a drunken, horny, naked beauty queen. There's something about the former Miss Firecracker that makes him want to blow his Mr. Nice Guy persona all to hell.

It helps that Willow is ready to dive headfirst into a no-heartstrings-attached affair. Which fits in perfectly with Blake's temporary gig managing his friend's bar.

Every grinding kiss, every stolen touch leads to another...until a harmless little white lie becomes the detonator that could explode their chances at a happily ever after.

Warning: this light-hearted beach read features a hero hotter than the 4th of July and a feisty heroine who knows exactly how to pop his top.

Look for these titles by
Lorelei James

Now Available:

Rough Riders Series
Long Hard Ride
Rode Hard, Put Up Wet
Cowgirl Up and Ride
Tied Up, Tied Down
Rough, Raw, and Ready
Branded As Trouble
Shoulda Been A Cowboy
All Jacked Up
Raising Kane

Beginnings Anthology: Babe in the Woods
Three's Company Anthology: Wicked Garden
Wild Ride Anthology: Strong, Silent Type

Dirty Deeds
Running With the Devil

Wild West Boys

Lorelei James

A Samhain Publishing, Ltd. publication.

Samhain Publishing, Ltd.
577 Mulberry Street, Suite 1520
Macon, GA 31201
www.samhainpublishing.com

Wild West Boys
Print ISBN: 978-1-60504-730-0
Mistress Christmas Copyright © 2010 by Lorelei James
Miss Firecracker Copyright © 2010 by Lorelei James

Cover by Natalie Winters

Mistress Christmas, ISBN 978-1-60504-274-9
First Samhain Publishing, Ltd. electronic publication: December 2008
Miss Firecracker, ISBN 978-1-60504-594-8
First Samhain Publishing, Ltd. electronic publication: June 2009
First Samhain Publishing, Ltd. print publication: May 2010

Contents

Mistress Christmas

Dedication

To my husband EJA: you're the best Christmas present ever!

Chapter One

"I look like an X-rated Mrs. Claus!" Holly North did a double take at her brazen image in the full-length mirror.

"That's the point."

"I don't think Santa would approve."

"*Au contraire.* I have it on good authority Santa loves naughty girls way more than nice girls. You should see what *they* get for Christmas."

"I can't wear this. My nipples are practically showing." Holly yanked up the red leather bustier.

Ivy jerked the bustier back down. "Leave it. Customers want to believe they're getting a free peep show."

Holly gaped at her friend, Ivy Lane, owner of Sugar Plums, a "gentleman's" club—aka a high-class strip joint. She gestured to the skintight leather pants, the shelf-like bustier that displayed her boobs like Christmas ornaments, and the four-inch poinsettia-red stilettos. "No man out there is going to buy that I'm the infamous Mistress Christmas, regardless if I'm wearing the costume."

"It's all in the attitude, sweetums." Ivy frowned and tugged the black leather pants to Holly's hipbones. "Actually it's in the hips. Swivel 'em, baby."

"Great." Holly stared at the exposed section of her stomach where the bustier and the pants gapped. She turned sideways.

Truthfully, she didn't look half-bad. Pilates three times a week kept her belly from jiggling like a bowl full of jelly.

Still...as she stared at the smoky-eyed, half-naked stranger in the mirror, she wondered if she should've skipped that last glass of mulled wine. How could she even consider parading in public dressed this way?

"Just cop an attitude. Rule number one: sell yourself," Ivy intoned. "Stop acting like an accountant."

"But I *am* an accountant." Ivy was her best pal—and top client. When Holly had impulsively stopped by to drop off quarterly tax forms, Ivy had pleaded with Holly to cover Mistress Christmas's shift. Not only was the real Mistress sick, half of the bartenders and bouncers were out sick too.

Since Sugar Plums was a Christmas-themed strip joint, the club was especially swamped during the holidays. And since Holly was a sucker, she had a hard time saying the word *no* to her desperate friend.

But a teeny part of her was excited to break out of the boring mold and act bold and daring.

"You are a damn good accountant, Holls. However, you are also one gorgeous woman." Ivy slathered on the flattery as thick as Tom and Jerry batter. "You shouldn't hide this hot, curvy body under tweed, wool and prim looks. Shake it. Flaunt it. I guarantee my customers are gonna eat you up."

Holly's eyes widened. "But you said I wouldn't actually have to get on stage and dance. I can't strut around like a holiday dominatrix! What if someone recognizes me?"

"Trust me, I barely recognize you." Ivy sighed. "Anyway, you don't have to strip. And it's not like I expect you to do lap dances. We'll announce you, you'll walk across the stage and then you'll mingle with the customers."

"That's all?" she asked skeptically.

"Yep. You can come back to the dressing rooms and chill between Divinity's and Candy Cane's sets, if you want." Ivy rummaged through a cardboard box of props, muttering to herself.

"Aha!" She waved a red velvet mask at Holly. "Put this on. It'll give you an air of mystery and a measure of privacy."

"Fine." Holly slid the mask over her face, careful not to smear the artfully applied makeup or jostle the tinsel threaded through her hair. The minute that sinfully soft velvet caressed her skin, Holly's modesty miraculously vanished.

Wow. She didn't look like Holly North, respectable accountant; she looked...like a complete sexpot.

Oh yeah. This could be fun. Freeing.

Getting in the holiday spirit, Holly smiled coyly at Ivy in the mirror. "Hand me the red lipstick. Do you think I should dust snowy glitter across my cleavage? Or would that be too much?"

❖

Detective Nick West sipped his Artic Ale and scrutinized the interior of Sugar Plums. Classy joint. Dark, but clean. The place could use a few more bouncers—security was a bit lax in his opinion.

The sound system pulsed and the strobe lights flashed in time to music heavy on the bass line. Although the stage was empty, the place was packed with single men, outrageously priced drinks in hand, their hungry gazes glued to the trio of brass stripper poles center stage as a disco ball spun, casting a kaleidoscope of color across the white walls.

To the left was a screened-off area that Nick assumed was for lap dances—not that he knew about those firsthand. Strip clubs had never been his thing, even in his younger years when he was raising hell in Wyoming with his notoriously wild McKay cousins. And luckily, early on in his career, Adult-oriented businesses—or AOBs—weren't on his patrol assignments.

To the right was another small but open room, which housed the video lottery machines. Several overweight guys sat in front of the glowing blue screens, in a daze, poking buttons and feeding money into the greedy bill slots like junkies.

What a waste. A spark of anger reminded him why he was here. Last week his friend Rudy Donner had spent an evening at Sugar Plums. During a lap dance, the stripper known as Mistress Christmas had drugged his drink and lifted fifteen hundred bucks from his wallet. Rudy didn't remember much besides waking up in his car, cold, hungover and dead broke. Poor Rudy had been too embarrassed to press charges.

So Nick decided he'd check the place out on his own time, off the clock. He'd get up close and personal with the mysterious Mistress Christmas. If she pulled the same shit on him, well, he'd slap a pair of cuffs on her faster than she could say, "Merry Christmas, Officer." And his cuffs weren't the velvet-lined novelty type she was probably used to.

The music ended abruptly. An air of expectation filled the room and all eyes focused on the door on the stage.

A throaty female voice boomed over the stereo system. "Let's get this party started! First up tonight, for your pleasure, we have the talents of Divinity, followed by Velvet and lastly, the ever-popular Candy Cane. To get this party going, I'd like to introduce Mistress Christmas."

More whoops resounded.

"Mistress Christmas isn't dancing this evening."

Boos ensued.

Nick frowned and a suspicious feeling rolled through him. What kind of strip club was this that the headliner wasn't dancing?

"Now don't get your jocks in a knot, boys. Instead of shaking her Christmas bon-bon, she'll be out front mingling with all of you, sharing her special brand of holiday cheer. Let's give Mistress Christmas a big Sugar Plums welcome!"

Wolf whistles, catcalls, and wild applause rang out as the lights dimmed. The door opened and out stepped a vision of pure sex on stilettos.

Holy shit. The woman was a goddess. Tall and built like a brick shithouse. Her leather-clad legs went on forever. Her tits weren't the enormous jugs most strippers displayed, but rosy mounds that filled out the skintight corset to perfection. Her lips were full, lush and crimson stained. Her auburn hair, threaded with glittery tinsel, cascaded down her bare back. A mask covered half her angular face, accentuating her wide eyes and pouty mouth.

Visions of those red lips sliding up and down his cock, striping his dick like a candy cane, made his cock stand at full attention.

Jesus. No wonder this woman had suckered Rudy. She was an absolute wet dream.

She spun, twirled and strutted, playing her part to the hilt. Acting coquettish—the type of woman who'd purr like a kitten in polite company, but roar, scratch and bite like a tigress behind closed bedroom doors. The type of woman Nick secretly craved.

After several long minutes of watching every man in the joint approach her, Nick drained his beer and stood. No way was any other man putting his hands on her. No. Fucking. Way.

Tonight, Mistress Christmas belonged to him.

Holly took her time sauntering across the room to the

horseshoe-shaped bar, smiling, flirting, acting like she knew what the hell she was doing.

Time dragged on, and after fifteen excruciating minutes, she needed a booster shot of liquid courage. She'd barely curled her fingers around the brass bar rail when warm breath tickled the damp skin below her ear. "Buy you a drink, Mistress Christmas?"

A chill trickled down her spine upon hearing the sexy masculine drawl. Holly half-turned. Good thing she held the railing because the man crowding her was the most spectacular male specimen she'd seen since...well, since *ever*.

Merry Christmas to her.

He was big; at least an imposing six-foot-three, and his body appeared to have been crafted out of solid muscle. His golden hair brushed the collar of his plaid western shirt, which stretched across his shoulders nearly as broad as the bar top. Laugh lines creased the corners of his hazel eyes, as well as the corners of his captivating lips. Lips that were curved into a big ol' shit-eating grin.

Oh mama. That lethal smile could prove to be her downfall.

"Did I pass your inspection, darlin'?"

"With flying colors." So much for acting cool and professional. She regrouped and smiled cheekily. "I believe you mentioned something about buying me a drink?"

"Absolutely. What's your pleasure?"

You. "I'm in the mood for peppermint schnapps."

"A taste of sweet and sticky coming right up."

He scooted close enough she could differentiate the varying shades of gold, blond and brown in his wavy hair. And the scent of him was intoxicating—clean linen and hot man.

When he reached across the bar, the inside of his thick

wrist grazed the bared skin below her ribcage. The electric shock of the simple contact nearly buckled her knees. A little gasp of surprise escaped before she could stop it.

His frown was there and gone as he paid the bartender and slid two shot glasses within reach.

When Holly faced him fully, his gaze focused on hers with an intensity that caused her eyelashes to tingle. As she attempted to gulp down her shot, he placed his warm, rough-skinned hand atop hers, stilling the motion.

"Ah ah ah. Not before we toast."

"To what?"

"Come now, I'm sure this isn't the first time you've made a toast in here."

How wrong he was. Holly racked her brain for a clever phrase. "How about...to Christmas wishes coming true?" Heaven help her, this man appeared to be everything she'd ever wished for.

"Don't you think that's a little vague, Mistress Christmas?"

Lord. His sexy voice was as dangerous as his sexy smirk. She managed, "Do you have a specific wish in mind?"

His burning gaze raked her from the tips of her pointed ears to the tips of her pointed nipples. "I've got a very explicit wish. Would you like to hear it?"

Her body vibrated as if he'd whispered *very explicit* across every inch of her passion-soaked skin. "Maybe you should tell me your name before we start sharing wishes and dreams."

"Nick."

"Hmm. Are you anything like your namesake, Saint Nick?"

"Not even close, darlin'. I'll offer no apologies that I've always been more sinner than saint material."

"You do have that devilish look about you, Not-So-Saint

17

Nick."

Nick stared at her mouth, virtually growling, "I like the way my name sounds tumbling from your sweet lips."

Playing with fire, Holly.

But she wasn't brainy Holly North, shy accountant. She was bold Mistress Christmas, embodiment of sexual fantasies. And she'd milk that persona, live the dream of being the object of men's physical desire, if only for a single night.

Holly lifted the glass to her mouth and ran her tongue around the rim, licking at the thick liquid clinging to the edge. The man's gaze darkened; another thrill zipped through her. "Where'd you learn to talk so sweet?"

"Wyoming."

"Does that make you a real cowboy?"

"Yep. Born and bred, dust on my boots, sage in my blood, dyed-in-the-wool gen-u-wine, native Wyoming hell-raiser." He raised his glass to hers. "You impressed?"

"Very."

"So let's toast to overcoming first impressions."

Weird toast, but she smiled. "I'll drink to that."

They chinked their glasses and knocked back the schnapps.

Holly welcomed the sweet fire flowing down her throat and slammed the empty glass on the bar with a heartfelt, "Ah."

"Another?"

She automatically started to decline, but her inner vixen cooed, "Why not?"

"Coming right up." Nick signaled the bartender.

The next shot boosted Holly's confidence. "Tell me, Nick, if you're really a cowboy, where's your hat?"

"Same place as my horse—at home in Wyoming."

"Do you live there?"

"Nope. I'm riding a steel horse in Denver these days. What about you?"

"No hat or horse," she hedged playfully. "Not that it matters because I don't know the first thing about riding."

A twinkle brightened his eyes. "Really?"

She cautioned, "Before you ask, *no*, I don't want to save a horse and ride a cowboy."

"Pity."

Nick's you-caught-me-with-naughty-thoughts grin made her stomach cartwheel as fast as Wyoming tumbleweeds.

"I'd be more than willing to show you a few secret cowboy tricks once you mounted up."

"I'll just bet you could," she murmured.

"I'll just bet you were born to ride. You'd look amazing on top. Your thighs clamped tight, your back arched just so, your head held high as you find the natural rhythm of moving on a powerful body. This gorgeous mane"—he twirled a section around his index finger—"trailing between your shoulder blades as you buck bareback. Every part of you bouncing as you're pushing faster and harder, until you explode from the sheer joy of the ultimate ride."

Holly didn't dare look away from the sexual challenge in Nick's eyes, but she couldn't keep the heat from rising in her cheeks, nor from hearing her mother's warning: *If you keep playing with matches, child, you're gonna get burned.*

A mischievous grin tilted his mouth as he leaned forward. "You're awful quiet all of a sudden, darlin'. You okay?"

Smug man. If she were going up in flames, she'd drag Nick right along with her. "Oh, I was just thinking."

"About?"

"Something you oughta remember, cowboy. Not all women mount up the same or crave that type of wild ride. See, you're all about fast, furious, pulse-pounding action. I imagined a slower, sweeter pace for the first go-round. Taking time to learn the subtle signals before handing over the reins. Not rushing headlong to the glorious end, all hot and sweaty and tired." Holly bit her lip, as if deep in thought. A little buzz fizzed in her blood when Nick's gaze zoomed to her mouth.

"I'd prefer drawing out the excitement. Gliding along with abandon. Building the pace one step at a time until that moment you dig your heels in and break free, reveling in the rush of an unbridled, unbound, rigorous ride."

Nick just blinked at her and then he swallowed hard.

Hah. "You're awful quiet all of a sudden, darlin'," she teased. "You okay?"

"You're good at that."

Holly cocked her head saucily. "Good at what, cowboy?"

"Reminding me you're a professional."

A professional? What the hell? *He'd* started it.

"Hey, shweetheart, lemme buy you a drink," a man slurred behind them.

She froze. Indulging in verbal foreplay meant she'd neglected her mingling duties with other customers. She shouldn't have allowed one hot, sexy Wyoming cowboy to monopolize her time and attention.

Before she addressed the man, Nick stepped in front of her and snapped, "Back off, buddy. The lady is occupied."

Boozy breath sliced the air between them. "You can't just act like she's yours—"

"Yes, I can, because tonight, she is."

The DJ's voice cut through the music. Conversation around them stopped. "Gentleman, come closer because it's time for a sweet treat from Miss Divinity."

"Take a hint." Nick loomed over the guy. "Or do I hafta spell it out for you?"

"No. We're cool. I'm going." The man held up his hands.

Another round of whoops rent the air as Def Leppard's "Pour Some Sugar on Me" blasted from the speakers.

Nick and the man automatically looked to the stage.

Holly needed a moment to clear the effects of the booze and of this domineering man from her addled brain. Seeing his distraction, she ducked around another portly patron and hightailed it past the bar, vanishing behind the screens.

Chapter Two

Nick made sure the drunken asshole was good and gone before he turned around...only to find Mistress Christmas gone as well.

What the hell?

He scanned the crowd surrounding the stripper on stage. No sign of Mistress Christmas. Why'd she pull the disappearing act when he'd set himself up to be an easy mark? Nick figured after knocking back shots on his dime and teasing him to distraction, she'd be raring to kick it to the next level: a private lap dance.

His lower gut muscles knotted as he imagined her rubbing that sweet, round ass across his crotch. Seeing her tits swaying as she shimmied her chest in his face, bringing her nipples close enough to taste. The bump and grind coupled with that sexy lip-biting thing she did? Whoo-ee. It'd be damn near impossible not to explode in his jeans and maintain professional restraint.

Man. Mistress Christmas was good. For a while he'd almost believed she'd stuck around because she liked him, not because she was being *paid* to like him.

Talk about being pegged a sucker.

But her vanishing act didn't make sense. She'd hooked him; why didn't she reel him in?

Frustrated, Nick skirted the bar and headed toward the privacy screens. There she was, arguing with a spandex clad bouncer who looked like an escapee from the *WWE Smackdown!* Neither one noticed his approach.

"—the big deal is?" she asked.

"Just following instructions, Holly."

Holly. Hmm. Was that her real name? Or a holiday-themed alias to fit with the atmosphere?

"But I'm not going to—"

"Sorry to interrupt"—Nick flashed a quick smile—"but I wondered where you'd wandered off to. We have some unfinished business to attend to, darlin'."

The bouncer pivoted. "This is a private conversation. Scram."

"Doesn't look private. Nice costume." Nick let his gaze wander up the green tights covering the man's tree-trunk sized thighs, and across the red sports shorts and the matching green and red striped T-shirt. "What superhero are you supposed to be?"

"I'm not supposed to be a superhero, lame brain. I'm supposed to be an elf."

"Whoa. Doncha think you're a little big to pull off the elf gig?"

"I think if you don't watch your smart mouth I'll put my big elf boot straight up your smart ass."

"Stop it. Both of you."

Nick clammed up, keeping his comment about the differences between bells and balls to himself. Getting thrown out of here on his ear by Santa's monster helper wouldn't help Rudy.

"You want me to get rid of him?" the gigantic elf demanded.

She shook her head.

"Who is he? Do you know him?"

"Sort of. Actually I, ah, met him earlier, and I ah...promised him..."

"What?"

Without meeting Nick's eyes, she blurted, "A lap dance."

"You?" The bouncer scowled. "Does boss lady know about this?"

"No. And I'd prefer to keep it that way."

What was Mistress Christmas hiding from her boss? Evidence she'd been ripping men off? Was the bouncer in on it?

Mr. Red and Green Spandex barked, "Remind him of the rules. If he breaks them, I break *him.* Understood?"

Mistress Christmas nodded and snagged Nick's hand as she tugged him around the privacy screen that provided a silhouetted image of the clandestine couple to feed other bar patron's voyeuristic tendencies. The shadowed tease of a feminine form in motion was far sexier than the strippers on the stage wearing nothing but skin, in Nick's humble opinion.

The two main areas were empty. He supposed the prime time for lap dances was between a stripper's sets. Mistress Christmas led him to the far corner, which was too far back to be part of the free peep show.

Essentially they were alone.

One low-slung, padded wooden bench was the only furniture in the space. A boom box with a long extension cord had been propped in the corner.

"Have a seat, cowboy."

Nick sat, hooking his heels on the outside edges of the bench. "What rules was he talking about?"

She spun toward him. "You mean you don't know?"

"No." He laughed. "Will you believe me when I confess I'm not a regular patron of clubs like these?" *Come on, baby, take the bait.*

Her dazzling smile rivaled the glow of the light display strewn across the ceiling. "I believe you. But the truth is, I didn't intend to go through with the lap dance thingy anyway."

Thingy? Not the lingo he'd expected from a hardcore professional stripper. In fact, there were more than a few things about Mistress Christmas that just didn't add up.

"—pawing me and I just needed to get out of there for a minute. I'm sure you understand, since you're not used to these types of establishments."

So she'd decided to play that angle? Nick could almost hear her canned speech: *This is such an awful place. I hate working in a strip club, even when it's temporary. I'm trying to get out of this life. I'm not like the other girls who work here. From the first time I saw you I sensed you were different and you knew I was different. Might sound crazy, but I like being with you because you make me feel safe.*

Right. As if he'd buy that.

And then Nick knew he had to demand the lap dance. To see how far she'd take the role of the big-hearted, misunderstood stripper. He dug in the front pocket of his jeans and pulled out a wad of cash.

Her eyes widened before they met his.

"I like bein' with you too. Which is why I'm gonna hafta insist on that dance, darlin'."

"What?"

"See, that's why I ventured into this strip club in the first place. A buddy of mine was here last week and he said you were the hottest woman he'd ever clapped eyes on. He told me you damn near melted his clothes to his body with the sexy way you danced."

"But—"

"I wanna get me some of that dirty dancin' as my own special Christmas treat. Or should I say Christmas wish?"

She didn't respond.

"So how much?" Nick waved the money and waited for the greedy Mistress Christmas to appear.

Holly panicked. How was she supposed to get out of this? Nick actually believed she was a stripper.

Well, duh, Holls, you're in a strip club dressed like a dominatrix. What's he supposed to think? That you're an accountant from Cherry Creek?

Maybe she could reason with him. Ignoring the rigid set to his jaw, she said, "Look, I think you might've gotten the wrong idea about me. Let's talk to the manager. She'll set you up with someone else."

"I don't want anyone else, *Holly*"—he paused, giving her a second to absorb the fact that he'd heard her real name—"I want you. Just you. No substitutions."

She saw the challenge in his eyes. Nick expected her to argue. He probably didn't even care about a damn lap dance; he just wanted her to refuse so he could cause problems.

Screw that.

The schnapps provided enough edge that his high-handed behavior pissed her off. Rather than back down and return to being Holly the wallflower, she threw her head back and became Holly the wallbanger.

Not-So-Saint Nick wanted her to dance? She'd dance. And he'd pay for it in more ways than one.

Holly smiled seductively. "A private lap dance will cost you one hundred bucks."

"That's pricey."

"I'm worth it."

"Prove it." Nick peeled off five twenties and attempted to place the money in her palm.

"Ah ah ah. Roll the bills up together and hold them between your lips like you're puffing on a cigar."

"Do you know how dirty money is?"

"Do you know how dirty I can dance?" she countered with a husky purr.

His eyes flashed interest, fire, and she knew he'd totally forgotten about potential germs.

"While I'm picking a song, put your hands by your sides and wait for me to decide where I'll allow you to place the payment."

She strolled to the boom box and flipped through the CD selection. Lots of smoky blues tunes. Boring. If she planned to follow through with this and play the femme fatale to the hilt, she'd pick a song he'd never forget. A song that'd make him hard as an icicle every time he heard it. She paused when she reached a familiar cover.

Perfect.

Holly's hands shook as she started the CD. Now she just had to remember the sinuous moves she'd seen other strippers perform. The ballet lessons she'd stopped taking twenty years ago weren't ringing a bell, but she'd watched enough episodes of *Dancing with the Stars* to fake it, right?

Her nerves zipped from fear to fire when she heard the distinctive *tick tick tick tick* followed by the grinding guitar riff *baum badabaum badabaum* of AC/DC's "Back in Black".

Throwing her hips out side-to-side in a sexy manner as she

sauntered forward was harder than it looked. She must've been successful. Nick couldn't keep the rolled bills between his lips because his jaw had dropped.

Heh heh.

Nick hastily picked up the cash and put his money back where his mouth was.

Holly allowed a brash grin as she gyrated her hips to the escalating drumbeat. Placing her hands on his shoulders, she stepped between his knees and angled her chest beneath his jaw. "Put the money in the right side of my corset. With your teeth."

A male sound of approval emerged as he bent his head. His silky hair brushed the tops of her breasts, soft as a lover's whisper and she bit back a sigh.

His ragged exhalations drifted across the perspiration coating her skin as Nick oh-so-slowly pushed the slender cash roll down the center of her cleavage.

The second his whiskers scratched her mounded flesh, Holly saw a challenging glint in his eyes. "I can't get it in all the way, darlin', without using my hands."

Ooh. What a cocky comment. She hitched her shoulders sideways, forcing his chin to graze both her breasts. "Maybe you oughta use your tongue, *darlin'*, since it's the strongest muscle in the body."

Nick placed the tip of his tongue alongside the money roll and pushed it beneath the cup of her bustier, licking the hidden swell, damn near touching her nipple.

A wave of desire washed over her and she forgot to breathe, and swayed a bit from the dizzy sensation.

"A little wetness always makes it glide in easier, doncha think? Especially since this is bigger than what you're used to." He jammed his tongue in again, withdrawing the wet warmth before sliding the money down and out of sight. His hair floated across her collarbones, releasing his dark and alluring male scent. After placing a gentle kiss on the top button of her bustier, he traced a path up the center of her cleavage with openmouthed kisses, heated breath, and the rasp of his beard.

Lust slammed into her and she almost came right then.

Not good, remind him who's in charge.

Holly nudged his face up with her sternum and swept her damp lips over his ear, whispering, "Now be a good boy and I'll show you why Santa begs me to sit on his lap." She spun around and began to shake her groove thang.

He groaned when she rubbed her leather-clad ass up the inside of his thigh, stopping at the junction of his legs.

While keeping her arms above her head for balance, she made little grinding circles on his crotch. Over and over. Swinging her loose hair across his handsome face so strands caught on his razor stubble and tickled his pouty lips. Holly slid her butt cheeks up the inside of his other leg, swishing her hips back and forth. Dropping her arms, she situated her hands on his knees. She peeped over her shoulder, rocking her pelvis until once again her ass was nestled against his groin.

Nick's obvious erection sent a gush of moisture to her core, causing her to taunt, "Is that a jumbo candy cane in your pocket or are you happy to see me, Not-So-Saint Nick?"

A feral snarl rumbled from his mouth and his hands latched onto her hips. "Keep it up and you'll get more than you bargained for."

Holly refused to let his challenge go unmet. "Maybe you're already getting more than you bargained for." Once again her arms twisted above her head like a belly dancer's. She rotated her shoulders, shimmying and scraping her backside against that rock-hard flesh pressing beneath his jeans. Her heart thudded. Her skin was hot and tingly. Her nipples were hard as gumdrops.

Nick's rough thumbs stroked the bared section of her skin peeking above the waistband of her pants. "Jesus, you're killing me. Harder." He pressed her bottom more firmly to his crotch.

A yelp escaped as her spine landed against the solid wall of his chest. He snaked her left arm around the back of his neck, and threaded the fingers of his left hand through her right hand. Not an inch of space existed between them.

Then Nick fisted his hand in her hair and pulled her head to the side so his mouth could attack her throat with demanding kisses.

"Oh God." Nothing set her off like lips and teeth and tongue on that sensitive section of her neck. She automatically writhed against him, desperate for more.

His pelvis was bumping up, as hers ground down, and they moved from side-to-side in perfect synchronization. His hot, wet mouth destroyed any sense of decorum and she moaned with utter abandon.

Swearing, Nick pushed her away, spun her around, and aligned her body until they were face-to-face. He draped her legs the opposite direction of his on the bench. The friction at this angle was perfect. Pelvis-to-pelvis, her clitoris rubbed the seam on the inside of her pants and the bulge in his jeans. The soft mounds of her breasts were plastered to his hard chest.

Lift, lower, grind. Lift, lower, grind.

So close. Dammit. It'd been a year since she'd experienced a climax not brought about by her own hand. She craved that explosion. That mindless throbbing. That ultimate rush of heat.

"Holly." Nick groaned her name like a prayer and clamped his hands to her face. He slammed his mouth to hers in a ferocious kiss that stole her breath, her sanity and sent her careening over the edge straight into orgasm.

She kept moving, dragging out the delicious sensation. Then Nick stiffened below her and she felt a burst of warmth where they were pressed together.

He rode out his climax. A growl-like hum reverberated in her mouth, as he soul-kissed her so deeply she swore the steady movement of his tongue tickled the soles of her feet. When his thumbs simultaneously stroked the edge of the velvet mask and the curve of her cheek beneath it, she damn near came again at the simple eroticism in his tender touch.

Nick released her lips, kissing the line of her jaw to her ear. Breathing hard, he murmured, "Now I finally understand the appeal of lap dances."

Then it hit her: she'd been dry-humping a complete stranger in public.

Talk about cheap.

What you mean cheap? He paid you a hundred bucks for the privilege of getting his rocks off with you.

Holy crap. Holly scrambled off him like he'd suddenly developed a case of leprosy. She fell on her ass before she leapt to her feet.

"Holly? What's wrong?"

"Nothing. Everything. Shit. Shit-shit-shit-shit-shit. *Shit.* I have to go. Now." She backed away, trying—and failing—not to stare at the dark, wet patch on the front of his jeans.

"No, wait."

She didn't. Holly turned and fled through the door backstage where she knew she'd be safe. But she didn't know if she was running from him or from the bad-girl wild side of herself that scared her to death.

Fuck.

Mistress Christmas had gotten him so hot and bothered from a simple goddamn lap dance that he'd squirted in his jeans. It'd been years since he'd had to untuck his shirt to cover the evidence of an accidental discharge.

Stunned, Nick sat on the bench and replayed the entire encounter. What a damn enchantress. From Holly's come-hither smile, to the sexy, mesmerizing motions of her smoking hot body, to the sound of her breathy sighs, she was absolute perfection. He licked his lips, once again tasting the hunger and neediness in her kiss.

None of that kissing, full-frontal grinding should've happened. The "hands off" policy for lap dances in strip clubs was usually strictly controlled. The stripper taunted and teased, rubbed and gyrated, while the customer basically sat on his damn hands and watched. Nick knew those were the rules.

So why hadn't Mistress Christmas known them?

Granted, the sensuous way that womanly body of hers swiveled and shimmied was breath stealing, but there'd been something...sweet and unsullied about her performance. Something shy and earnest about her. A feverish need to please that seemed to surprise her as much as it had him.

But Nick had to ask himself—could innocence be faked? Was that how she lured men to financial recklessness? Get the bouncer to look the other way, break the "rules" about no touching, bring the customer to orgasm while faking her own? Then the stripper with the heart of gold runs away, expecting the customer to be so desperate to get off again in secret that he'd come back for more?

He could totally see that angle working. Problem was, he couldn't see Holly as the type of woman to work that angle.

Which was probably why it worked so goddamn well.

After Nick retrieved his coat, he scrutinized the bar for a glimpse of her.

Nada.

Cold air and snow blasted him in the face when he stepped outside, but it didn't cool his temper or his libido. With nothing else to occupy his time, he could wait in his car in the parking lot and hope to see her sneaking out the employee entrance.

Yeah? What then? Follow her? To what end?

Nick needed to catch her in the act of stealing inside the bar, not stalk her to see if she lived in a low-rent district. Not fantasize that she'd welcome his advances outside the club.

Jesus. How pathetic did it make him that he didn't have anything better to do than moon over a stripper who'd given him the first decent orgasm he'd had in over a year?

Nick's pager buzzed. He read the text scrolling across the screen. Figured. Duty called him back to the station.

His gaze lingered on the vehicles parked by the service entrance before he drove off.

But he'd be back.

Chapter Three

"You ran out of here pretty fast last night, Holly. Was everything okay?"

"Uh. Yeah." Holly applied crimson lipstick to her upper lip.

"You sure? Bubba said you disappeared for awhile into the private area and then you careened back here like you'd seen your grandma in the audience."

The lipstick slipped, smearing a thick red line across Holly's cheek. "Goddammit, Ivy! That's not even funny."

"Jumpy much?" Ivy pinched Holly's chin between her thumb and forefinger and swiped at the streak. "What's going on with you?"

"Nothing." She couldn't share what'd happened with Nick with anyone, least of all Ivy.

Nick. Just thinking about the man sent an ache between her thighs. That cowboy was outstanding and out of her league with a capital "O" for orgasm—unintended or not. After the volatile lap dance, she'd hidden in the dressing room until she'd had to strut across the stage. And once again, it'd taken two shots of schnapps to bolster her courage.

Thank God Nick hadn't been around. She'd managed to flirt with several patrons before ditching her sexy, sassy persona and heading home.

After the way she'd bolted last night, chances were slim

Nick would be back. He'd gotten way more bang for his hundred bucks anyway. Her discussions with other strippers cemented her mortification. How was she supposed to've known there was no touching, no kissing and definitely no orgasms during lap dances?

Still, Holly had guts enough to face the naughty truth: even if she had known the rules, she would've done it exactly the same way. Dammit. How mortifying to have it bad for a man she'd met in a strip club? And she didn't even know his last name? Her attraction to him mattered not one whit, because if Nick found out she wasn't a hot-to-trot stripper, he wouldn't be interested in her at all.

"Holls, why is your face all red? You aren't getting sick, are you?"

"No." Holly jerked her chin from Ivy's hand. "It's from the glass of red wine."

"Thank goodness you haven't contracted the creeping crud floating around here. If I haven't already told you a million times, I'll say it again. Thank you for filling in again tonight."

"You're welcome. Remember this favor when it's tax season and I need an office drone."

Ivy grinned. "You've got it." She tugged the bustier down, so the lace barely covered Holly's nipples and handed her the velvet mask. "Same drill as before. Knock 'em dead."

The music started and Holly played her part, infusing the crowd with Christmas spirit. And truthfully, sitting at the bar surrounded by a dozen admiring men did wonders for her ego.

She'd even stopped scanning the crowd for a tall, well-built cowboy with golden curls and knowing hazel eyes. She remained among the patrons through the first two stripper sets and only ventured back to the dressing rooms before her last stage strut.

After she was announced and as she meandered past the first pole, she caught sight of that long, muscled body leaning against the closest wall. The heat in his eyes was powerful enough to ignite the fires inside her from twenty feet away.

In her distraction, Holly forgot to watch her step and stumbled over her own feet. Just when it looked as if she'd take a header down the stairs, Nick's apparent cat-like reflexes kicked in and he caught her fall from grace before she broke her neck.

"Hold on there, darlin'. I gotcha." Hands firmly gripping her hips, he steered her to an empty barstool. "You okay?"

"Um. Yeah. I'm fine."

Nick gestured to the bartender. "Bring her a glass of water, would ya?"

"Sure thing."

Holly perched on the edge of the barstool, hooking her heels on the bottom rung, trying to quell her racing heart. "You must think I'm a total klutz."

"Not in the least."

A heavy pause lingered as she sipped the lukewarm water from a plastic cup. Almost as an afterthought, she said, "I didn't think I'd see you tonight."

Those shrewd hazel eyes focused on her. "Why's that?"

She shrugged and studied the kaleidoscope of colors spinning across the walls by the stage.

"You wondering if I'm here for more of the same?"

"Even if you were, it wouldn't matter."

"Shame. I'd pay twice what it cost me last night."

Warmth suffused her cheeks beneath the mask. She downed the remaining water in two gulps. "Thanks for keeping me from falling on my face. But my gratitude does *not* include a lap dance. Of any variety." She stood without acknowledging him, even when the man cast a shadow across the width of the bar that was damn hard to ignore.

"Holly—"

"Mistress Christmas? Can I buy you a drink?"

Holly glanced at the weaselly man who'd snuck along Nick's right side. Plastering on a fake smile, she said, "Absolutely. I'm in the mood for a change of holiday scenery." She didn't lift her eyes any higher than Nick's muscular arm. "Excuse us."

For the next ten minutes the computer techie named Bart shifted from foot to foot, blathering on about nothing. Holly nodded in all the right places and moved on to the next paying customer. Through it all she felt the weight of Nick's stare. Or was it his disappointment?

When the last stripper stormed the stage, Holly took her leave. She hung up the costume, removed the heavy makeup and dressed in her clothes. Ivy was nowhere to be seen and Holly was grateful for the chance to sneak out the back door and get back to her real life.

Boring as that life might be.

Nick parked at the rear door, facing the employee entrance, close enough to catch Holly no matter which vehicle was hers, no matter what time she left.

Dammit. He wanted to kick his own ass for playing it wrong tonight.

No you don't. You went exactly by the book and she didn't take the bait.

Why hadn't she? Something definitely didn't fit. As his mind raced through a couple of scenarios, a bundled up figure exited and paused under the sodium lights.

Nick's breath stalled. The woman took two steps, slipped and fell right on her ass.

Yep. Had to be Holly.

He bailed out of his truck and barely kept himself from landing on top of her as he skidded to a stop on the icy pavement. He crouched down and those bright green eyes looked up at him. "You okay?"

"Nothing hurt but my pride, especially since that's the second spill you've witnessed tonight."

Nick held out his hand to help her. Soon as she was upright, she backed away from him, a hint of fear in her eyes. "What are you doing out here?"

"If I admit I was waiting for you will you think I'm a stalker?"

"Probably. So I'll warn you I have pepper spray and I know how to use it."

As a cop, Nick appreciated her caution. "Duly noted. I'm here to apologize for being an ass earlier. I'm sure you deal with a lot of jerks on a nightly basis and I'd hate for you to lump me in with them. I'm really not such a bad guy."

"Neither was Ted Bundy, or so he claimed."

He smiled. "So does that mean there's nothin' I can do to convince you to have a cup of coffee with me?"

A long, cold pause settled between them.

"What?"

"Why would you want to have coffee with me? I'm not really—" Holly snapped her mouth shut.

"You're not really what? Not really thirsty?"

She shook her head.

"Not single? Please tell me you're not married or involved with someone?"

Another head shake.

"Then what?"

"It's umm...probably against the company rules for me to meet customers outside of club business hours."

Probably? This woman confused the hell out of him. How could she not know company policy? "That spectacular lap dance you performed last night was probably against company policy too, but you don't see me tattling on you for that, do you?"

"No. But..." Holly squared her shoulders and got right in his face. "Why are you interested in me? As you can plainly see, I'm pretty plain without the sexy costume and hoochie-mama makeup."

Hoochie-mama? Lord, where did she dig up such terms? "Holly, the last thing you are is plain." Nick let his gaze encompass her entire face. "You have beautiful eyes, a beautiful smile and there's this...glow about you that doesn't have a damn thing to do with the stage lights."

"Are all Wyoming cowboys such sweet talkers?"

"From birth, darlin'. And we're honest as the day is long, too."

That comment brought a genuine smile to her face and he was completely captivated.

"Fine. One cup of coffee after you tell me your entire name."

"You want my rank and serial number too?"

"Have a nice life." She turned away.

Laughing at her cheekiness, he caught her forearm. "Sorry. It caught me off guard. My entire name is Nick Lander West."

Holly frowned. "Lander? That's weird."

"Evidently I was conceived in Lander, Wyoming, and my parents thought it'd be funny as a middle name. I figure it could've been worse, considering my brother Blake's middle name is Thermopolis."

"You're joking."

"Yes, I am." He grinned at her. "And fair's fair, darlin'. What's your whole name?"

She said, "Holly Jolly Christmas," without batting an eyelash.

Which caused Nick to roll his eyes. "Everyone's a comedian. I deserved that, I guess. Since it's getting colder, I'll allow the sleight of name until we're at the restaurant. How about if we meet—"

"Huh-uh, cowboy. *I* get to pick the place we meet."

Bossy little thing. "Deal. Where?"

Holly gave him a considering look. "IHOP on the north end of Spear Boulevard."

"Sounds good to me."

Neither one budged as they stared at each other amidst the swirling snow and flashing neon lights from the club.

"Aren't you gonna get goin'?" he prompted.

"Not until you leave."

"Why? Are you planning to stand me up?"

"No. But since I have your full name I also want to write down your license plate number so if something hinky happens to me the cops know who to look for and what vehicle you drive."

Nick laughed. Hard. If she only knew. On the back of his truck was the discreet sticker that allowed him to park in the police department's private garage. "To show you I'm trustworthy, I'll oblige you. But be warned, if you stand me up, I'll chase you down, 'cause, darlin', I know where you work."

He thought he heard her mutter, "Don't be so sure," but it

was probably a trick of the wind.

True to her word Holly did jot down Nick's license number. When she reached the IHOP parking lot she also peeked inside the window. If she saw rope, handcuffs, or duct tape, she was outta here.

But in all honestly, she wouldn't have agreed to meet him if she hadn't felt some semblance of trust when it came to Nick West. She wasn't naïve. Maybe she was a fool to fall for his "aw-shucks" Wyoming cowboy routine. She'd suffered through plenty of blind dates with less personal information and less chemistry.

Plus, she'd already had an orgasm with him, fully clothed, in public. How mind blowing would sex be completely naked in private?

Talk about coming unhinged. One minute she scoped his truck for signs of kidnapping supplies and the next she patted her pockets for condoms? She really needed to get out more.

Nick had chosen a booth against the windows in the middle of the restaurant. He stood when he saw her and helped her take off her coat.

"Thank you."

"No problem. I didn't order coffee because I wasn't sure whether you liked it."

"I live on it in my line of work."

"Me too," he admitted and signaled for the waiter.

After the coffee was poured, Holly leaned back against the fake leather booth. She steered the conversation away from her supposed job at the strip club and went on the offensive. "So, what do you do for a living?"

"Paperwork. Lots and lots of paperwork." Nick sipped his

coffee. "You gonna tell me your real name?"

"My first name really is Holly. My middle name is Anne. My last name is North, which is ironic considering yours is West."

"That is ironic. You from around here originally?"

"No. I'm from Connecticut."

"Wow. That's a ways away. You have family there?"

"Yeah. I hardly ever see them." It'd be safe to assume Nick attributed the estrangement to her occupation. Which in a way was exactly right, as she had nothing in common with her family any longer. "What about you?"

"Most of my family lives in Wyoming. My dad and my brother Blake raise sheep and my mom's job is to keep them from killing each other. Blake isn't married, although an epidemic of weddings has broken out in the last few years amongst my McKay cousins." He cocked his head. "What about your family?"

"One sister, one brother. Both married. Both living on the East Coast. Both popping out grandkids for my parents. So I'm the pariah out here in no man's land. They can't imagine why anyone would want to live in Denver and I can't imagine why anyone would want to live anywhere else."

"I hear ya. I love to visit the homeplace, but I don't see myself ever goin' back to Wyoming to live permanently."

"Not even because you miss your horse?"

His bad-boy grin was a thing of beauty. "Not even because I miss my horse *and* my hat."

"I'll admit I'd like to see you tricked out in chaps, spurs, a hat and boots, swinging a lasso."

Before Holly's chagrin for her suggestive comment set in, Nick grabbed her hand. He dragged his mouth across the inside of her wrist and the feel of his warm, soft lips created a swoopy sensation in her belly. "I notice you didn't mention me wearing pants of any sort."

"Nick—"

"Say my name again, all soft and breathy like that," he demanded.

"Nick, I don't know what I'm doing here. I've never done anything like this."

"Like what?"

"Meeting up with a man like you."

He frowned. "What do you mean, a man like me?"

"A man who is hot as sin, built like a Bronco's defensive end, and is confident enough to make me take risks I never had the guts to before. A man who can get me off fully clothed in less than five minutes. A man who makes me wonder..."

"Wonder what?" His eyes flared pure male interest.

"What it'd feel like to experience passion like that again, sans clothing of any sort." There. She'd said it.

"That was your first taste of passion?"

Holly shook her head. "But it's been awhile...a long while since I've experienced anything remotely close. In the last few days I've realized I'm still not living the life I envisioned."

"If you could change that vision, what would you do first?"

Here's your golden opportunity, Holls. Grab the bull by the horns and demand the cowboy take you for a ride.

"Remember when we toasted and you asked me about Christmas wishes?"

He nodded.

"I was too nervous to be honest about what I wanted."

"So be honest now. What is your fondest Christmas wish?"

"One night of sexual decadence."

Both his eyebrows lifted.

"With you."

Nick's jaw tightened. "Are you fucking with me?"

"If that means I'm propositioning you, then yes." Rather than retreat from his suspicious eyes, Holly leaned closer. "Aren't you curious to see how delicious it'd be to get off when we're naked together?"

"Like you wouldn't believe. But I've gotta ask why the sudden change of heart? How can you be sure I'm not a serial killer?"

"Because you would've followed me home from the club and snatched me on a deserted road, not bullied me into having coffee with you in public."

"True. So how do I make your wish come true, Mistress Christmas?"

"Don't call me that." Holly wrinkled her nose. "That's not who I am."

"Who are you?"

"A woman who's interested in you. So the question is, are you interested in me?"

Instead of answering, Nick placed her hand over his heart to show her how fast it beat.

The heat in his eyes, in his hand, in his body stoked the fire inside her hotter than she ever dreamed.

"Your chest is so hard," she whispered.

"And it ain't even the hardest part of me right now."

Holly smiled at his comment. "One night? No strings, no promises, no regrets?"

"Deal. With one little catch."

"Which is?"

"If it's up to me to fulfill all your sexual wishes, then I get to be one hundred percent in charge of providing that pleasure. You have to trust me and do what I tell you."

"Within reason. No pain games."

"I'm not into pain. I'm into seeing your body light up like a Christmas tree from all the orgasms I'm gonna wring from you." Nick kissed the tip of each finger. "Since you picked the restaurant, I get to pick the hotel." He paused, as if expecting her to argue.

She didn't.

"Marriott Suites on Lexington. Thirty minutes. I'll leave a key at the front desk under my name." Nick slid out of the booth and threw a five-dollar bill on the table. "Don't keep me waiting, darlin'."

"That's just around the corner. I don't need thirty minutes."

"I do, since I'll be picking up condoms and stuff on the way."

"What kind of stuff?" she said suspiciously.

Nick grinned. "Bet you were the type who peeked at your presents before Christmas morning, too."

She squirmed. Busted.

"You'll have to wait and see." He bent down until they were nose to nose. "Here's the God honest truth. I thought you were something special in that skintight leather-and-lace get up, mysterious and sexy. I gotta admit I prefer you natural like this, your hair loose around your face, wide-eyed, your breath ragged as you're waiting for me to kiss you."

Do it.

"I'm gonna demand to feel your soft lips all over my body, Holly. Can you handle that?"

Her pulse thumped like mad. She managed a little nod.

"Good." Nick brushed his mouth over hers until her lips parted. Then he blew her mind with a kiss so sweetly, so shockingly seductive she feared she'd come undone right there in the booth.

When he finally backed off, his voice was thick with desire. "Not nearly enough, but it'll hold me for the next twenty-eight minutes and fourteen seconds."

Chapter Four

As Nick purchased condoms and other accoutrements he needed, he wasn't thinking like Detective West, one of metro Denver's finest. Nick was purely thinking like a man about to get very, very lucky.

Yet, if in the course of having his wicked way with Holly he discovered information pertaining to Rudy's situation, so be it, he'd use it. But his gut told him Holly was exactly who she said she was: a woman out for a little sexual adventure.

Although, part of him had a hard time believing Holly couldn't have a date every night of the week if she chose. Especially since she spent nights surrounded by eager men.

Then again, Nick could see why hotsy-totsy Mistress Christmas intimidated most guys. They probably assumed she had so many offers they didn't bother to make one.

Luckily, he didn't have the same problem.

Nick plunked down the extra cash for an executive suite — with a whirlpool hot tub, complimentary champagne, and a California king-sized bed. The room even boasted a fully decorated Christmas tree.

Damn. Maybe Holly wouldn't want a reminder of her job.

Nothing he could do about it now. He kicked off his boots and wondered if it'd be crass to put the condoms and stuff on the nightstand by the bed.

No, it'd be crass if you spread them out all over the room where you hoped to take her—the mattress, by the chair, the back of the couch, on the counter in the bathroom, or the lip of the hot tub.

Yeah, that'd freak her out. He left the unopened box on the nightstand.

Nick checked the time on his cell phone again. Thirty-two minutes had passed since they'd parted ways at IHOP. She claimed she didn't need that much time. What if she'd changed her mind?

A rap sounded on the door, followed by the soft click of the lock disengaging. A shaft of light cut through the darkened room across the gray carpet.

Holly shut the door behind her and took a couple steps into the room and froze.

He froze.

They stared at each other over the five feet separating them.

"I was afraid you'd changed your mind," he said softly.

"I almost did." Her eyes searched his face. "I'm out of my element. I had no earthly idea when I propositioned you what I'm supposed to do once I'm actually standing here."

"Take off your clothes."

She blinked. "Seriously? Now? Just like that?"

"Yep."

"But—" She paused. "That's what you want, Nick? A striptease?"

"No." His hungry gaze swept her head to toe. "I'd rather tear your clothes off myself and fuck you hard and fast against the door, so I can take you slow and easy the second time on the bed. The third time is a toss-up between screwing you in the hot tub or bending you over the chair. But a striptease never crossed my mind."

She swallowed hard but she never looked away.

"Fair is fair, Holly. Now you tell me how you want it."

"Like that. Up against the door. My fantasy is you're so crazed to have me you can't wait another second."

"Not a fantasy, a reality." Nick's hands were in her hair and his mouth smashed hers before she took her next breath.

God, she tasted good. Sweet and hot. As he kissed her he herded her toward the door. He reached for the purse straps dangling from her fingertips. Change jangled and a thud echoed as he carelessly threw her purse by the desk.

Holly moaned.

Nick unbuttoned her coat and slid it off her shoulders, tossing it aside. His fingers traced the center of her body down to the bottom of her sweater. "Lift up," he urged.

She raised her arms and the woolen tunic crackled with static as he jerked it over her head. Her long-sleeved T-shirt followed.

He smoothed her flyaway hair and whispered, "There's some serious electricity between us, isn't there, darlin'?"

"Yes, it makes my skin tingle."

"And I haven't gotten started yet." The velvety swell of her breasts spilling over her plain white bra beckoned for a thorough taste. He nibbled the column of her throat until his chin nestled in her cleavage.

Her soft plea, "More, don't stop," amplified his level of lust. His fingers fumbled for the snap on her jeans and he eased the zipper down.

Somehow Holly managed to unbutton his shirt and her cool palms stroked his bare chest.

Nick skimmed his hands up her hips and spine. One quick tug on the hook of her bra and the cups fell away, revealing every marvelous inch of her breasts. "God, you're perfect," he said before sucking the pale peach nipple deeply into his mouth.

"Oh, that's good."

"Mmm," was his response as he suckled and nipped, using his teeth on the tip and lapping away the sting. Nick lavished attention on those delicious globes until she whimpered. As he kissed his way back up to her delectable mouth, his fingers slid down. His middle finger breached the panty barrier, following the sweet cleft down past her pussy lips, and found the heat and wetness of her arousal.

A throaty moan rumbled from her mouth.

"You're ready for me," he growled. "Kick off your shoes. Then take off your pants. Fast." Nick stepped back and peeled off his socks. He watched as Holly shimmied out of the denim.

She hooked her fingers in the waistband of her panties and paused.

"Unless you want me to rip them off, those too."

Holly honestly looked as if she'd prefer that action, which caused him to make another primitive growl. Her underwear vanished.

Nick reached in his back pocket for his wallet and removed the lone condom. He tossed his wallet somewhere in the vicinity of the desk and stripped his jeans off. After ripping open the wrapper with his teeth, he rolled the latex down the length of his shaft.

"Buried balls deep inside you, right now." Curling his hands around her butt cheeks, he said, "Hang tight," and lifted her against the door.

A surprised squeak escaped. Her legs automatically caught

his hips and her arms circled his neck.

He aligned his cock to that sweet, wet hole and gritted his teeth, aching to ride her hard from the start. But when he struggled to get the first couple inches in, he was relieved he'd ignored his baser impulses. Holly was unbelievably tight. He swallowed her mewling noises, working himself inside her little by little, until the gripping heat of her sex surrounded his cock.

As her body adjusted around him, he began to kiss her slowly, craving her surrender, heating her up to the point she melted into him.

Holly pulled his hair to break his lips free from hers. "Show me that passion. Fast and hard, Nick. Make me burn."

Holding her gaze, he withdrew and slammed deep. Three. Four. Five. Six solid thrusts.

"Yes. God. Just like that."

With his hands clamped on her ass, Nick continued to stare into her eyes as he flexed his hips. "I'm glad we've got all night because this first go-round is gonna be short."

"That's the only short thing about you, cowboy."

He placed his lips against her ear. "Now who's the sweet-talker?"

"Not sweet and no talking." She lightly bit his jaw. "Fuck me harder."

The next three plunges sent Holly into orbit. Her fingernails dug into his shoulders. Her pussy muscles tightened around his cock. Her head thunked into the door, exposing the long line of her throat.

Nick sucked on the tempting arc of her neck as she shuddered and moaned, her body thrashing against him and the door. He lost himself in her vanilla scent, the faint taste of salt on her skin and her unrestrained response.

When the last pulses of her orgasm faded, he lengthened his strokes.

So close. More. Dammit. No. He wanted this to last.

Her husky whisper, "Let go," amidst suckling kisses on his earlobe pushed him right into a sexual overload.

He pounded into her as his balls lifted, sending streams of liquid fire up his shaft. Nick squeezed his eyes shut, letting his inner beast take control, grunting his pleasure as her wet lips traced the straining cords of his neck. Her breathy murmurs tickled his ear, sending shivers dancing across his skin.

Nick's head spun. He could scarcely catch his balance or his breath, or absorb the reality of this soft, sexy woman trembling in his arms.

Eventually damp kisses tracking his hairline roused him back to planet Earth. "Nick?"

"Mmm?"

"Can you unstick me from the door?"

He tipped his head back and looked into her passion-glazed eyes. "In a minute. This first." Nick settled his mouth on hers and kissed with all the gentleness and sweetness he could muster.

When he released her lips in tiny, nipping increments, she sighed dreamily.

"You ready for the second item on my Christmas wish list?"

"I thought you were supposed to be fulfilling *my* fantasies, Not-So-Saint Nick."

"I am. But I think me tasting your sugar plum to my heart's content will fulfill both our fantasies, don't you?"

Holly's pliant body thrummed with anticipation as Nick carried her to the bed and laid her flat on the cushiony mattress.

"Sit tight. I'll be right back."

Her gaze swept the hotel suite. Nick certainly hadn't skimped. The room was a step above typical, even for a suite. The wall sconces emitted a soft golden light across the enormous bed and a Christmas tree glowed in the corner.

The toilet flushed. Water ran. The bathroom door opened.

Nick held a washcloth in his hand and wore a sheepish expression. "You sore? I...ah...was a little rough."

"I told you I didn't mind. It was exactly what I wanted." *You're exactly what I wanted* went unsaid.

He crawled next to her and pressed his lips to hers at the same time the cool cloth pressed against her swollen sex. Nick swallowed her surprised gasp and stroked his hand up her belly, smiling against her mouth when those sensitive muscles between her hipbones quivered. The tip of his thumb dipped into her navel, brushing circles around the indent and journeying upward. When he reached her ribs, she giggled and pushed him away.

"Stop."

"Ticklish?"

"Terribly."

"Will I hafta restrain you when I do this?" Nick's tongue traced the bend in her waist up to her armpit and under the lower swell of her breast.

"Nick!"

"What?" He did the same thing down the other side.

Holly tried hard not to laugh but it was hopeless. "God. That tickles."

Before she figured out the method to his madness, he'd moved and hung above her. He lowered his mouth until she could feel his rapid exhalations on her skin. Then that wicked pink tongue licked just the very tip of her nipple.

She completely forgot about laughing as she watched him lap circles around the distended tip. Each pass wider than the last. Wetter than the last. His eyes drew darker. His breaths more jagged. Oh she wanted that mouth closer. She arched her back, hoping he'd read the deliberate invitation.

His hazel eyes locked to hers. "No coyness allowed. Tell me what you want."

Holly clamped her hands on the side of his face. "I want you to suck on my nipples. On both of them. Hard. Make me squirm. Make me wet." Then she yanked his head down.

Nick did exactly as she asked. Suckling her so deep she swore her nipple hit the back of his tongue. He squeezed and fondled one breast, tracing the point across the top curve, teasing the underswell with his fingertips while working the other over with his mouth. He switched sides numerous times and seemed to take immense pride in her every twist, every whimpering, begging moan.

She'd never come so close to orgasm from a man taking such enjoyment strictly from her breasts.

His head lifted. "I made you squirm. Now let's see if I can make you wet."

"You already did."

"That's what I wanna hear." He removed the washcloth and kissed down her belly to the center of her body. Upon reaching the single, almost invisible strip of reddish-brown curls on her mound, he grinned. "It's like an arrow pointing to my destination. Handy." Large hands landed on the inside of her thighs. "Spread 'em. I wanna taste every inch of this bare-skinned pussy."

Heat flooded Holly's face. It was hot as hell, hearing Nick

call a spade a spade—or a pussy a pussy, in this case. She flexed her heels and slid them across the satiny sheets as wide as she could reach.

"Damn, woman." Nick's eyes were molten with desire. "You are flexible. I bet I can bend you every which way, can't I?"

"Probably."

That gorgeous cowboy grin flashed. "I fully intend on testing that theory later. For right now..." He thoroughly licked the length of her slit, groaned deeply, smacked his lips as if he'd tasted ambrosia and did it again. And again.

When Holly bumped her hips for more, he stopped, gazing at her across the naked length of her body.

"Huh-uh. No fast get-off. I'm taking my time. You'll come when I'm ready for you to come, not until. And when you do come"—he jammed his tongue inside her channel and wiggled it before withdrawing completely—"you'll scream my name."

Her whole body trembled. "But, Nick—"

"No negotiations. Hands above your head." His eyes twinkled. "Or you can play with your tits. Your choice."

Her legs went rigid as his head disappeared between her thighs again.

"Lord, what it does to me to see this sweet cream dripping down faster than I can catch it," he mumbled against the crease of her thigh.

That naughty tongue mapped every crevice. Every hidden fold. He suckled her pussy lips, letting his teeth lightly graze her clit. He repeatedly kissed the strip of hair, rubbing his chin and cheeks over it, almost...marking her. He kissed, licked and sucked every smooth section of her freshly waxed skin.

Her stomach fluttered. Her whole body burned hot. Even her damn toes twitched with pleasure. There wasn't a doubt in Holly's mind Nick enjoyed driving her to the brink and was memorizing her reactions and filing it away for future use.

For future use? Wishful thinking, Holls. This is a one-night-only deal. Tomorrow morning you'll both walk away chock-full of fully realized triple X-rated Christmas wishes.

Her enthusiasm sagged at the thought of not seeing the sexy, raunchy Not-So-Saint Nick again.

When he bit the inside of her knee, she gasped, "What was that for?"

"I lost you there for a second. Thought I might be boring you."

Holly propped herself up on her elbows. "Not bored, just figuring out the best way to beg you to finish me off."

"That'll do it. Lay back. I've gotcha."

She moaned when Nick gently latched onto her clit. He hummed over that bundle of nerves, sending a fresh set of shivers rippling through her body.

A finger slipped into her wet channel. At the added stimulus and the feeling of fullness, she expelled a soft, appreciative sigh. Nick chuckled and inserted another finger.

When he did a swirly flick over her clit, she couldn't help but pump her pelvis and whisper, "Please."

As Nick stroked the spot inside her sheath underneath her pubic bone, he fastened his lips around that protective hood and sucked. And kept on sucking until her clitoris spasmed and her shoulders bowed off the bed as she ground her sex into his face.

Holly's body had never known pleasure so sharp, a synchronized throbbing in her head, her pussy, her clit, and her nipples that made a mockery of her previous sexual experiences.

She tried to push Nick's clever mouth away even as she

clutched his head to hold him there forever. He didn't budge until the last twinge pulsed against his tongue. She sagged into the mattress, helpless to do anything but try to find her sanity, kick start her lungs, and formulate a decent marriage proposal.

Nick snickered against her pelvis. "That good, huh?"

"What?"

"You just asked me to marry you."

Holly jackknifed up. "Shit. I said that out loud?"

"Yep."

Talk about embarrassing.

He stood and reached for the unopened box of (magnum sized!) condoms on the nightstand and she couldn't help but stare at him. Drool, really. Wonder if she ought to buy a lottery ticket because, hot damn, it was her lucky night. Fully clothed, Nick was magnificent. Completely naked, he was flat-out a god.

A god who'd had his face buried between her thighs for the last twenty minutes.

Definitely lottery ticket material.

Nick ripped open a condom and had it rolled on before she cleared the fog of lust from her sex-addled brain.

"...on one condition."

She managed to tear her gaze from his impressive hard-on (two erections? in thirty minutes?) and met his eyes. "Umm. Sorry. I didn't hear all of that. What did you say?"

He flopped on the bed beside her. "I said any woman I marry needs to know how to ride." He brushed the hair from her face. "So mount up and show me whatcha got."

That telltale warmth spread across her cheeks again. "But I—"

"Goddamn it's a turn on to see you blush."

Holly's gaze dropped to his groin. "Doesn't look like you

need any help in getting turned on."

"All your doin', darlin'." Nick placed his hand in the middle of her back and urged her forward. "Straddle me."

Nerves had her biting her lip as she threw her leg over his, startled by the molten heat radiating from his body.

Nick swept her hair away from her face and tilted her chin up. "Holly? What's wrong?"

She blurted, "I've never done it this way before."

Pause. "Well, you're just loaded with surprises tonight." Nick twined a section of hair around his finger and tugged her closer. "Kiss me. I can't get enough of this mouth."

"But what about—"

"We'll get there. No hurry." Nick gave her another slow, bone-melting kind of kiss. Complete with long, sweeping caresses of his work-rough hands up her legs and torso, over her shoulders and down her spine to her buttocks. He didn't push or pull her toward his erection. He seemed content to touch her and learn every nuance of her mouth.

Holly slipped her lips free from his and flicked the sexy dent in his chin, loving the rasp of his stubble against her tongue. She used her teeth to nip the intriguing angle of his jawbone until she reached his ear. "I'm ready for my riding lesson, cowboy."

He chuckled. "Scoot back. Feel me?"

"You mean that big, hard, thick thing sticking up?"

"Again with the sweet talkin'. When you're ready, pop 'er in and commence to ridin'."

"That's it?"

"Yep. You set the pace. You're in charge."

"Do I sit up? Or lay across you?"

"Either way. If you sit up I can reach your clit. But I ain't gonna complain about having them beautiful tits rubbing on my chest."

She rose on her knees, aligned her pelvis to his and held the rigid shaft straight up with one hand as she braced her free hand on his broad chest. Heat darkened his eyes as he watched his cock slowly disappearing into her body.

Holly took her own sweet time and was pleased Nick didn't grab hold of her hips and force her down.

Once he was fully seated inside her, he closed his eyes and groaned. "Ah, hell. You feel good, Holly. Warm and tight and perfect. I could get used to this."

Nick's sweet words gave her pause.

"You okay?"

"Are you?" she countered.

"Never been better. Do what you want, darlin', you have the reins."

She experimented with lifting and lowering. Loving the deep push at the end. But she missed that skin-on-skin contact. She angled forward, placing her hands beside his head and shimmied down. "Oh."

"Like that do you?"

"God yes."

"Let me help. You'll like this even better." Nick grabbed onto her butt cheeks and squeezed, gently rocking her.

"Oh, that's...I really like that."

"Thought you might. Don't tense up. Another good thing about you laying in this position? I can kiss you and run my hands all over your soft skin."

Holly rocked on him, amazed by the sense of power of being on top. Amazed by the control Nick freely handed over. Amazed by how his lazy, wet kisses were deceptively seductive. She hadn't had many lovers in her twenty-eight years, and none of them showed this trust and playfulness, sometimes even after months of dating, that Nick had shown her in just a few hours.

He kissed his way down her throat. "Whatcha thinkin' about so hard, darlin'?"

"Sorry. I-I tend to overthink things." She quit moving on him. "Are you mad?"

"No. Just curious as to what drew your attention away from this." He flexed his hips. "'Cause it's mighty fine."

She groaned. "It is. I was thinking about you. How much...you don't mind that I'm not...you're so patient... You're just so great and I'm really happy to be here with you."

"Holly. Baby." His voice was gruff. "C'mere."

Nick's kisses intensified and she began to push back onto all that male hardness. Sliding belly to belly. The scrape of his chest hair on her nipples sent shudders down her spine, which he chased with fingertips soft as raindrops.

The continual graze of his pubic hair on her clit brought forth a short, but powerful orgasm that left Holly gasping as she ground against him. He muttered against her throat, nonsensical masculine words of encouragement through every sweet pulse.

He fastened his hands to her ass and thrust up. "Right there. Just like that. Yes." Nick arched his neck and she eased back to watch his face as the orgasm washed over him. God he was sexy, lost in the moment, a moment of passion she'd brought to him. Another feeling of sexual power emboldened her to scatter kisses across his chest.

He blinked his eyes open with a small, surprised smile. "Whoa."

"I'll say. Does that mean you want me to stop?"

"Never." He followed the outline of her jaw with a shaking

fingertip. "I think you like being on top."

"Mmm-hmm. I think you've created a monster."

"Just wait until you see what I've got planned for the hot tub."

Chapter Five

"There's a hot tub in here?"

Lord, Nick loved Holly's wide-eyed look. Innocent, yet interested. "More like a deep bath with whirlpool jets." He toyed with her hair. "Sound like fun?"

"Everything sounds like fun with you." Holly smooched his nose and slid forward until his softened cock slipped from her body.

"Where you goin'?"

"To get a drink." She winked. "All that ridin' worked up a powerful thirst."

Nick grinned. "Would champagne quench it?"

There was that owl-eyed expression again. "You bought champagne?"

"Came with the room. You up for a glass or two?"

"Absolutely."

He hopped off the bed. "Let me clean up while you take the bottle of bubbly out of the fridge."

As soon as he stood, Holly wrapped her arms around him from behind and nuzzled the middle of his back. "Thank you."

"For?"

No response, but as she'd burrowed deeper into him so sweetly Nick didn't press her for an answer. He merely squeezed her arm and said, "You're welcome," before continuing on to the bathroom.

When he returned, soft music drifted from the TV through the closed cabinet doors. Holly had donned a complimentary hotel robe and was curled up in the corner of the couch with her feet tucked beneath her. Strange. He'd expected nakedness wouldn't bother her. To set her at ease, he snagged the other robe she'd draped over the back of the chair.

She pointed to the bottle and glasses on the coffee table. "I'm not so good with things that have the potential to explode. It'd be just my luck if the cork hit me in the eye."

Nick loosened the wires and peeled the foil back. A couple of deft twists, a loud pop sounded and the cork released. A thin tendril of steam ghosted from the neck of the green bottle as he poured the sparkling liquid into the glasses.

"You're good at that. Popped a few tops in your day?"

Handing her a glass, he sat beside her. Right beside her. "The only top I'm interested in blowing is yours, darlin'."

Holly blushed and ducked her head. "I think we've established you're an expert in that area."

"Hey." He tipped her chin up. "Regrets?"

"Not a single one."

"Good. Then let's toast. To Christmas wishes coming true."

"I'll drink to that." She chinked her glass to his and downed every golden drop as he struggled to finish his mouthful.

"Like champagne, do you?"

She held the glass out for more. "Mmm-hmm. I tend to be a glutton since I never get it."

"Don't you have guys clamoring to buy you whatever drink your heart desires every night at Sugar Plums?" After Nick said it, he wished he'd kept his fool mouth shut.

Her cute freckled nose wrinkled. "No offense, but can that place be off the topic for discussion tonight?"

"Sure. As long as you answer one question for me first."

She squinted at him suspiciously. "What?"

"Is Christmas your favorite holiday?"

"No."

"No?"

"I mean, it's okay, and my attitude isn't because of work. There are so many expectations with that time of year. Buying the perfect gift for everyone on your list. The pressure to sacrifice vacation time to be with your family, and then once you get there you're sorry you ever came. The constant temptation to eat too much, to drink too much, to spend too much."

Nick stared at the liquid fizzing in his glass. "Or you end up spending it alone, wondering if everyone is having terrific family bonding time and you're some kind of pathetic loser because no one wants to spend Christmas with you."

"Exactly."

Their eyes met in perfect understanding and it floored him. Holly was the first person he'd run across who didn't wax poetic about the joys and wonders of the holiday season. The first person who'd understood his ambivalence.

"I take it you'll be alone this year?"

"Yes. You?"

"The same." He lifted his glass. "So what is your favorite holiday?"

"The Fourth of July," Holly said without pause.

"Really? Why?"

She shrugged. "The weather is hot. The beer is cold. Kids get just as excited seeing a fireworks display as they do seeing

Santa Claus. It lasts one day and there's usually a fair around."

"You like country fairs?"

"I'd never really been to one until I moved here. What's not to like? There's always tons of yummy bad-for-you food. Dizzying carnival rides. Pie eating and greased pig contests. Admiring the quilters' displays, watching the tractor pull and the demolition derby."

"Darlin', I'd love to take you home to our county fair. It's all that plus a rodeo. You'd have a blast."

Holly sipped the champagne and studied him in a highly unnerving manner. "You wouldn't be embarrassed to take someone like me back home to Wyoming?"

"What do you mean someone like you?" Then it occurred to him he'd been so comfortable with her that he'd completely forgotten Holly earned her living taking off her clothes. Not that he gave a crap what other folks said. "Hell no I wouldn't have a lick of embarrassment taking you home to meet the folks and neither should you. What you do for a job ain't all you are, Holly. I'd be damn proud to have you on my arm at the community rodeo dance."

"Pity I don't dance."

His glass stopped halfway to his mouth. "Run that by me again?"

She froze. "Umm. I meant, I don't couples dance. I've never been very good at it."

Nick offered a wolfish grin. "Well, it's your lucky night, 'cause I'm about the best two-stepper this side of Cheyenne."

"I imagine you are, but I'm hopeless."

"Never know unless you try." He pointed at her glass. "Drink up and the lesson will begin."

"Nick—"

"No arguing. This is my fantasy." He snatched the remote and changed the station.

Holly stood. "Your fantasy is teaching an uncoordinated acc—" Her mouth snapped shut. "Can't your fantasy be something simple and male like me giving you a blowjob in the hot tub?"

"Definitely a possibility for later. Right now my fantasy is two-steppin' naked with a beautiful woman." Nick held her gaze as he untied the belt on her robe. The lapels hung open, exposing her from chest to knees. He slipped his fingers beneath the nubby fabric to reach her smooth, warm skin and he gently pushed the robe off her shoulders. It landed on the carpet with a muffled thud. "Your turn."

Holly pressed her mouth to the hollow of his throat and made quick work of the knot keeping his robe together. The fabric slithered down his back and pooled on the floor.

Nick led her to the center of the room and clasped her left hand in his right, bringing her flush against him. He centered his left hand in the small of her back. "Comfy?"

"No. I feel stupid."

"Wrong. You feel great." Nick kissed her, amazed by the way her mouth floated over his in sweet surrender. Now if he could get her body to move like that, she'd be a two-steppin' sensation in no time. He'd love to take her to the western bars in the metro area. As they swayed together, he kissed her, lost in her.

When the song changed to a peppier beat, she balked and broke the kiss. "Wait."

"You're doin' fine. Easy as falling off a log. Step, step, shuffle back. Step, step, shuffle back. Step, step, shuffle back."

Holly dipped her head to stare at her feet and he nudged her chin back up.

"Eyes on mine. Feel the rhythm in the way your partner moves you, not in your feet. Every partner is different."

"How many partners are you preparing me for?"

Only me. Rather than answer, Nick pulled Holly closer as he took bigger, faster steps.

She eased forward the same as he did and she stomped on his foot. "Sorry. Good thing I wasn't wearing shoes."

"No biggie." He circled the room twice and the song ended.

Holly let go of his hands. Or tried to but Nick held tight.

"What's wrong?"

"Aren't we done?"

"We're just getting started."

Her laugh didn't quite reach her eyes. "I don't think so." She jerked free of his hold. "While I appreciate you taking pity on me for my lack of grace, we both know the chances of us ever dancing together after tonight are slim."

"Is that right?"

"Yep." She crossed her arms over her naked chest and notched that stubborn chin higher. "I didn't come here for dancing lessons. I don't want to spend the little time we have together cutting a rug like Bobby and Sissy. I'd rather be getting rug burns all over my body from you showing me what you really fantasize about."

Stung, Nick retorted, "Remember you said that when your knees are on fire." He lunged for her, spinning her so her delectable ass was nestled against his fully erect cock. He braced one arm across her shoulders and the other hand held both her wrists in front of her body. He ground his cock into her soft flesh, feeling victorious when she gasped.

"Just dancing with you has that effect on me."

"Nick, I didn't mean—"

"—to hurt my feelings? You did. Since you spurned my dance advances I've a mind to let you make it up to me. Luckily I've conjured up plenty of other fantasies starring little ol' you. And since you insisted on putting me in charge, we're gonna start out with one I like to call 'the cowboy's Christmas captive' or 'trussed up like a holiday turkey'. And no, you don't get to argue, 'cause, darlin', you're gonna be gagged."

Nick's grip around her wrists was like iron. Yet when she wiggled, he loosened it slightly, letting Holly know he didn't intend to hurt her, just play with her a little rougher than she was used to.

The thought of being bound for Nick's pleasure, at Nick's mercy, only able to voice her needs in nonverbal noises, made her absolutely dripping wet.

"You like that idea, doncha?"

When she didn't respond he put his mouth on her ear and demanded, "Answer the question while you still can."

Hot breath, hot man and his hot words caused a shiver and she hissed, "Yes."

Warm lips followed the arc of her throat down to her shoulder. "Good. I don't trust you not to run, so we're both gonna walk over to where I've stashed my supplies. Once I've got you how I want you then the real fun will begin."

Nick marched her to the nightstand and rummaged in the drawer. The sound of him rattling the condom box notched her excitement higher, made her pulse pound faster. Then they shuffled forward, stopping at the back of the couch.

He turned her around. Three bandanas dangled from his fingertips. His eyes never left hers as his hands worked at waist level.

Holly gaped at the twisted configuration. "Holy crap. You

did that without looking?"

"Yep. Did I mention I'm wicked good with anything that can be tied together?"

"Umm. No. You didn't."

He allowed a quick grin. "My mistake. Hold out your arms."

Concentration filled Nick's eyes as he looped the bandanas around her wrists, leaving about an eight-inch gap. Two quick tugs and a smug look appeared.

"Next comes the gag. But first..." Nick cupped her face in his hands and kissed her. Inhaled her, really. A tongue-thrusting tease that left her dizzy. Aching. Silly man could've just skipped the restraints and held her captive with the power of his mouth.

Then he touched her. Tracing the curve of her neck. The line of her collarbones, the slope of her shoulder down her back, his thumbs digging into the arc of her spine. The caresses were so sweet and loving that the rapid, sharp slaps on her ass shocked her, causing her to jerk back.

"What the heck?" barely slipped out before Nick had the other bandana stretched in her mouth. He spun her. A quick pinch and it was secured at the back of her head.

Nick wrapped his arms around her, once again putting his lips dangerously close to her ear. "You're mine now to do with as I please. Let's see whatcha look like with this beautiful body stretched out for my pleasure."

Holly chomped the fabric as Nick maneuvered her into a ninety-degree angle. Her body shook, partially from strutting around buck-ass nekkid, but mostly from the thrill of Nick's mysterious bondage game.

"I left you enough leeway in those restraints so that you can grip the back of the couch."

Her reply became a muffled moan when his palms slapped

the inside of her thighs. "Mmm-mmm would you check out all this sweet Holly juice? Thick and creamy. Makes a man mighty thirsty." Nick pressed his face next to hers. "Know the sexiest spot on a woman's body? Besides this sweep of skin where her neck meets her shoulder?" His rough fingertips danced over the area he'd described.

Gooseflesh spread across Holly's skin.

"The dimples above her ass. Those two sweet little indentations just beg for a man's undivided attention." He stood and his thumbs caressed her lower back. "This spot right here."

Her body twitched hard.

"Don't move. No matter what. Stay just like that."

Nick's heated touch vanished and was replaced by the cool brush of his mouth and the wet slash of his tongue.

The involuntary arch of her spine earned her a sharp slap on the ass.

"I said don't move." His free hand snaked up her belly to her breasts. He plucked and twirled the left nipple until it was pebble-hard and then he pinched it to the same beat he tapped on her throbbing clit.

All that stimulus, plus the licking and lapping across the sensitive base of her spine, made it difficult to stand still. Nick's every exhalation stirred the baby fine hair covering her lower back and she trembled violently.

"So sexy. So daring. So beautiful you steal my damn breath."

She wouldn't have been able to speak even if she hadn't been gagged. His words rumbled over her skin, adding another layer of arousal to her over-stimulated body and mind.

"I want to feel you come completely undone at my touch. I wanna hear you scream."

Holly tried to say, *too much*, but it came out a mumbled mass through the cotton covering her mouth. Nick moved and in her peripheral vision she saw him waving the bottle.

"There's not enough left for a full glass, so I might as well put it to good use." He dumped champagne into the small of her back.

A few droplets splashed on her shoulders, but the majority pooled in the well she'd created by keeping her pelvis tilted. Slurping soft kisses and the nip of teeth were the final straw to snap her obedience.

Holly bucked upward, sending the fizzy champagne trickling along the crack of her ass. The icy coldness did nothing to cool the burning between her thighs.

Nick's hands landed solidly on her butt cheeks and he pulled them apart as his warm tongue traced the cleft, chasing the trickles down where no man had ventured . He licked with feral groans of delight that reverberated up the length of her spinal cord and nearly set her hair on end. His tongue tickled, teased and probed. Her pussy. Her clit. Her anus. Never staying in one place long enough to get her off, just tightening the connection between all three hot spots.

Just when Holly knew she couldn't take any more, just when she suspected her knees would give out, Nick curled one meaty hand around her hip and impaled her.

The gag kept her from crying out.

Slam. Retreat. Slam. Retreat. Slam. Retreat.

Nick fucked her like he meant to imprint her body with the force of his. Hard. Relentless. No words. No sounds except for the *slap slap slap* of his hips connecting with her buttocks and his male grunts.

Wiggling had no effect. He was one hundred percent in charge of her pleasure. She couldn't verbalize her needs. She couldn't touch herself to hasten the race to orgasm. She couldn't even squeeze her legs together and increase the friction where she most needed it.

Without faltering in his rhythm, Nick slid his hand over her hip and began to lightly stroke her clit, which was in direct opposition to the unyielding way his cock rammed into her.

The contrasts were as staggering as the realization that in just a few short hours he'd established his mastery of her body.

When that deceptively gentle rubbing on her clit unleashed her orgasm like a tidal wave, he fisted his free hand in her hair, loosening the gag. "Now let me hear you."

She released her pent-up breath in a half-scream/half-wail.

Nick sank his teeth into the nape of her neck and sucked through every pulsing hot spasm of the most overwhelming, most intense, most perfect orgasm of her life.

Soon as he knew she'd reached the end, he straightened and gripped both her hips in his hands to better anchor his pounding thrusts. She felt the tip of his cock jerk inside her and a guttural moan burst from his mouth.

Holly bore down, clenching and unclenching around the male hardness, milking every twitch, wishing she could feel the heat of his ejaculate soothing the swollen tissues of her innermost walls.

Breathless, Nick slumped against her back, but she was so shaky she couldn't hold them both up.

"Hey. I've gotcha." He braced his arms beneath her. "You okay?"

"My arms are numb."

Nick chuckled and kissed the back of her head, reaching down to remove the bindings around her wrists. "Then we're even, because my dick is numb."

"I think you broke me."

"Yeah? I think you're more resilient than you're letting on." His breath ruffled the damp hair by her ear. "You sore?"

"A little."

"I could kiss it and make it better."

Holly snorted. "In light of our injuries I think we should call it a night and crawl in bed."

"Oh, hell no. We'll take it easy for a bit, but there's still a lot of night left. Still a lot we haven't tried, especially since we've gotta fulfill all those wicked and wild fantasies of yours before dawn."

A little whimper escaped. Because she couldn't take more of his fulfillment? Or because she didn't want the night to end?

Chapter Six

Nick couldn't believe he'd tied Holly up. He couldn't believe she'd let him gag her. Hell, he couldn't believe how hard he'd fucked her.

So he was a little nervous about what he'd see in her eyes when he faced her. Fear? Regret? Embarrassment?

Rather than dwell on it, Nick removed his semi-hard cock from that snug channel with a soft hiss. He wrapped his arms around Holly's midsection and buried his nose in her hair. God she smelled heavenly. Like vanilla. Like sugar cookies. Like home.

She sagged against him with a sigh.

A sigh was good. "You hungry? I could order room service."

"It has to be like two in the morning. I'm sure the restaurant isn't open."

"That's probably true."

"Are you hungry?"

"Always. But not hungry enough to leave you here alone while I track down food. Maybe I'll venture to the vending machine later." Nick kissed the top of her head. "For now, I'll start the bath." He retreated to the bathroom.

After ditching the condom, he flipped on the faucets for the garden style tub. As he washed his face and hands he heard a loud knock on the door.

Holly poked her head in. "Sorry to bug you, but can I sneak in the shower? I'm all sticky from the champagne."

"I'll join you. Especially since it was my doin', getting you all sticky." Before she protested, he opened the glass door and dragged her inside. He cranked the water on, keeping his back to the spray until it warmed up.

"Nick, we shouldn't—"

"We should. Don't think of anything but how my hands feel on your skin. Just think of this. Of how well we fit together. In so many different ways." Nick brought Holly's arms up to wreathe his neck. He slid his lips over hers, allowing his hands to wander over her slippery curves as he positioned her so the heated shower spray landed on her back.

He caught her sigh of satisfaction and pulled it deep into his lungs, filling his body and soul with her sweetness. The leisurely sweep of his hands became a silent promise that this time he'd take it slow. And he did. He kissed her and teased her and touched her to his heart's content.

Holly tugged on his hair.

"Mmm?" he said, letting his mouth skim the water droplets from the column of her throat, sucking the heady taste of her mixed with the water, knowing it'd do nothing to quench his thirst.

"Shouldn't we check on the tub to make sure it isn't overflowing?"

"In a sec."

"I'm serious. What if it's spilling over the edge and soaking the carpet? And dripping water into the room below us—"

"Relax. It'll be fine." Nick cupped her breasts and pushed them together so he could tongue both her nipples.

She trembled and a low moan drifted from her parted lips.

When he sank his teeth into a beaded tip, she gasped.

"Does that hurt?"

"No. Ah. Just the opposite. With those nips and bites I can almost..."

"Can you come like this?"

"I-I don't know."

"Then I'm gonna make it happen." Nick purred against her slick flesh. "God, I love your tits. I know that ain't politically correct, but these beauties are so damn tempting."

He gorged himself on the taste of her, the feel of her, her uninhibited response as she bumped her hips closer to his. The whimpering moans vibrating from her chest traveled to his lips and straight to his cock.

A particularly high-pitched gasp burst from Holly's mouth. "Harder. Nick. Please."

Without missing a beat, he sucked and tweaked the left nipple hard as she began to come. Nick looked at her, her head thrown back in abandon, completely unaware of the water pounding on her as she greedily took all the pleasure he offered.

When she expelled another one of those sexy, dreamy sighs, he licked his way back up her throat. "How was that?"

"Different." Holly opened her eyes and smiled at him. "No need for that ego to flare in defense. It was good different. A very good different since I've never had that happen before. It wasn't the same type as when you were sucking on my..."

He lifted a brow. "Your what?"

"You know." She blushed harder. "Made my whole body tingly."

"I could get used to making you tingly." Nick captured her mouth in a thorough kiss and reached behind her to shut off the shower. "Probably we'd better go check on the tub."

"Omigod. I totally forgot!"

"Then I must've been doin' something right. Come on," he said, grabbing her hand.

Holly bit back another sigh as she followed Nick's muscular naked body into the main part of the bathroom.

Nick kept hold of her hand as she swung her legs over the ledge and sank into the steaming water. "Ah. This is the perfect temperature."

"But it is a little full. Maybe I should do a cannonball to get rid of the excess water."

She cocked her head at him. "I wouldn't recommend it."

Laughing, he climbed in with total grace. "But I want you to be impressed with my cannonball skills."

"Trust me, I'm plenty impressed with your other skills."

"Yeah?"

"Yeah."

"So you don't wanna hear about the summer nights I spent at Keyhole Reservoir with my brother and my cousins? Having cannonball contests to see who could get the girls the wettest?"

Hands down, Nick got her the wettest of any man she'd ever known and he didn't have to perform a cannonball to prove it. Would he think she was lame if she mentioned it? Or would he laugh? She loved to hear his laugh.

"You're thinking too much again. C'mere." Nick brought her onto his lap, pressed her back to his chest and nestled her butt in his groin. He stretched his arms across the lip of the tub and her head fit perfectly in the space between his shoulder and his neck.

With the lights dimmed, surrounded by hot water and hot

man, another sigh slipped free.

"Comfy?"

"Mmm."

"Want the jets on?"

"Do you?"

"Maybe for a bit."

"Whatever you want."

His breath tickled her ear. "Why is it you're so accommodating?"

"You sound surprised."

"I guess I am. I sorta figured in your line of work, being front and center all the time, that you'd be more of a diva."

Holly snorted. Diva. Not exactly a word used to describe an accountant. But her body slumped when she realized Nick wasn't talking about her real career, but her supposed wild life as a stripper. Another mental snort sounded.

Come clean with him, he'll understand.

Right. Part of her thought he might accept her as Holly, the woman hot with numbers, but a larger part suspected it was Holly, the hot number, who held his interest.

"Holls?"

Lord. No one but her closest friends ever called her that, and it tickled her to hear the endearment coming from him. "I thought you were gonna turn on the jets?"

"I was until you sorta drifted off. Thinking too much again?"

"No. Just relaxed."

"Good. Jets coming right up."

Bubbles frothed and Holly closed her eyes, wondering if the water temperature, the sexual satisfaction, or the man's silent, comforting presence allowed her to loosen up so thoroughly. Her body went boneless. Nothing existed except the humid scent of the water, the *blub blub blub* of the whirlpool, and the quiet strength of the man holding her.

After a while the timer dinged and the jets turned off. She arched her back and her butt pressed into the erection that hadn't deflated a bit since they'd been skin-to-skin in the shower.

"More bubbles?"

"No. I'm good."

"You wanna get out?"

"Why're you being so accommodating?" she teased.

"Because I've got a beautiful nekkid woman plastered against me. Brings out my chivalrous side." Nick kissed the spot below her ear. "It's a part of my personality I usually keep hidden."

"Why?"

"Don't we all have aspects of ourselves we don't share with the world at large?"

Holly shrugged. "I guess."

"So...tell me something about yourself that no one else knows."

That was an odd request. "Why?"

"It'll be fun hearing your deeply hidden thoughts."

"If I share, that means you will too?"

"Yep. Turnabout is fair play. Come on. Tell me a secret."

She frowned. "A secret like I stole a piece of candy when I was five and never got caught?"

"Is that true?"

"No. I've never stolen anything in my life." Was it her

imagination or did Nick's posture stiffen?

Lightly, he said, "I was actually thinking a juicier tidbit. You know. Like you secretly jump on a trampoline in your backyard nekkid. Or you spent a weekend at a nudist colony. Or you went skinny-dippin' in the neighbor's pool when he was out of town."

"Why am I naked in all your scenarios?"

Nick trailed his hand from the tip of her fingers to her forearm, across her bicep in a sensual glide. Her skin rippled beneath his slow and steady touch. "Because I like picturing you nekkid, even when you're already nekkid in my arms."

"I hate to disappoint you, but I haven't done anything nearly that daring." She paused, half-afraid she'd disappoint him if she didn't confess to an outlandish and stripper-worthy scenario.

"Nothin'? Come on, spill it. I ain't gonna judge you."

"Well. This one time? At band camp?"

He chuckled against her neck and it sent tingles down her front, her back and everywhere in between.

"Smarty-pants."

"The truth is, you've got the wrong idea about me, Nick. I've never done anything wild. This"—her gesture incorporated the bathroom—"being here with you, having sex with a perfect stranger, is the most adventurous thing I've ever done."

She suspected his silence meant he didn't believe her.

"Seriously. I'm hopelessly square."

"I beg to differ." Nick smoothed his palm over the line of her hip. "There's not a square thing about you. You're all exquisite, tempting curves. I could just eat you up, sweet darlin'."

"Didn't you already do that?"

"Once ain't enough." He squeezed her ass between his

powerful thighs and his cock twitched against the small of her back. "Not nearly enough."

Her stomach knotted, remembering the surety of his mouth as he'd licked and slurped her to a frenzy. She wanted to give him the same mindless satisfaction he'd given her.

Feeling daring, she floated to the other side of the tub.

"Was it something I said?"

Holly nodded.

"What?"

"You said turnabout is fair play."

Liquid heat sparked his eyes.

"So, why don't you park that sexy butt up on the edge and let me have a chance at eatin' *you* up."

Didn't have to ask him twice. Water sloshed over the rim of the tub as Nick climbed into position.

Holly glided back and kept her gaze on his cock. When she licked her lips and wrapped those slender fingers around the root...he almost shot all over those delectable breasts.

She didn't tease. No soft licks. Or tormenting breaths. No seductive nuzzle of his sac. Or whispering kisses up the length of his shaft. Holly just swooped down and swallowed him whole.

"Jesus."

Her head bobbed fast. Her hand stroked faster. Her pace was relentless. Determined.

And fast. Way too fast.

Amazing as it felt surrounded by that tight, suctioning heat, she was going after him with such zeal he was on track to the speediest orgasm ever.

Was that her intent?

Nick nudged his thumbs in the hollows of her cheeks and stopped the motion. "Holly?"

Holly's expression read pure panic as his dick slipped from her mouth. "What? Am I doing it wrong?"

"No. God no. It's just...what's the hurry?"

Crimson spread across her cheekbones and she ducked her face from view. "Sorry."

"Hey. No reason to be sorry."

"It's just...I've never been very good at this sort of thing."

That softly spoken admission damn near ripped all the air from his lungs, mostly because he knew it'd been hard as hell for her to admit.

Or she was lying.

Damn the cynical part of his brain. "Can you look at me?"

She shook her head.

"Please?"

Again, she shook her head.

Nick fisted his hand in her hair and forced her chin up. Not a lie in her eyes, just pure humiliation.

"Listen. You didn't do a goddamn thing wrong. I love what you're doin'. Every suck. Every lick. Every stroke. That mouth of yours is wickedly good. But I wouldn't mind if you'd take it a little slower." He traced the pouty swell of her bottom lip with the center of his thumb. "I sure like seeing these full, pretty lips stretched around my cock. I love the feeling as you're takin' me deep into this hot, wet mouth. I love the way you curl your tongue under the sweet spot beneath the head when you pull back.

"It's sexy as shit having you on your knees in front of me. That's why I want you to go slow. Because I wanna savor it, Holls. This first time of you lovin' me with your mouth means too much for it to be over so quickly. And at the rate we were goin'...it was almost over when I stopped you."

"So you didn't stop me because you were disappointed in my technique?"

"Oh hell no. I'm just embarrassed to be so quick on the trigger." Nick gave her a sheepish smile and pushed a silky section of hair behind her ear. "You're in charge, but have pity on me, darlin', 'cause I'm the one with no control when your sweet, hot mouth is on me."

His confession appeared to soothe her. She offered him a sassy smile. "I'm really in charge?"

"Yep."

"Does that mean I can do whatever I want?"

"Within reason. No pain games."

"I'm not into pain. I'm into seeing your body light up like a Christmas tree with the orgasm I'm gonna wring from you."

He murmured, "Touché."

Holly kept her bright eyes on his as she leaned down and swallowed him again, but as she slowly released him, she scraped her teeth up his length with just the right amount of pressure, balancing on that deliciously sharp edge of pleasure and pain, before she freed the tip with a soft *pop*.

"Holy mother of saints."

She chuckled and the vibration zipped up, like his dick had become a lightning rod. Holly began a game of tease and retreat. Sucking. Backing off to paint his purple cockhead with little whips of her wet tongue. Then swirling her lips over the thick ridge separating the stem from the tip. Breathing on the damp spots, sending a rippling quiver up his belly as her fist jacked him off. The humming, sucking sensations danced across his skin like fire.

Then she'd stop, nuzzle his inner thigh and start over again.

Was she aware her firm grip at the base of his dick acted like a cock ring? That he teetered on the brink, craving that molten blast of release, only to be jerked back?

Nick watched her reveling in the power, almost as if it were a new experience.

Nah. Couldn't be. Holly held men enthralled every damn night. She was used to power.

Wasn't she?

When Holly looked up at him from beneath lowered lashes, his balls drew up hard as chestnuts.

"I'm gonna...you don't have to..." Nick could scarcely get the words out and he stopped his hips from bumping up.

"Don't you dare deny me. Give it to me. All of it. Now." The hand circling the base of his cock loosened and moved in tandem with Holly's bobbing, intensifying the pressure of her mouth.

"Oh. Yes. Like that. I'm fixin' to... Fuck!" Nick clamped his hands on Holly's head and slammed deep as wave after wave of come pulsed out his twitching cock and coated her tongue.

The roaring in Nick's head was as loud as the whirlpool jets had been earlier. Once he was fairly sure he wouldn't slip into a coma and drown, he slumped back against the wall with a drawn-out sigh.

Water splashed as Holly retreated.

He missed her warmth and the touch of her hand on his body. Nick's eyes flipped open.

A cute set of lines wrinkled her forehead as she squinted at him. Wariness stayed on her face, in her eyes, as she kept backing away.

Nick slithered into the tub and stalked her. "You're running out of places to go. And I don't understand why you're trying so hard to get away from me anyway."

"I-I..." She licked her lips. "Did you like that?"

"I loved it." He hauled her into his arms, pressing their upper bodies together. Man. He went half hard again at the sensation of those heavy breasts rubbing against his bare chest. "I kinda got the impression you liked doin' it."

Holly nodded against his neck. "It shocked me you weren't in a hurry to get off. Every time I've done it before, it's been like, get me off, or get me close to the point so I can stick it in you."

"Been with some real winners, haven't you?"

"Yeah." Holly's lips glided across his collarbone. "Will you think I'm some kind of freak if I admit I haven't really had that much experience in the...ah...dating world?"

"How much inexperience are we talking here?"

She shrugged.

"Darlin', you brought it up." Nick lazily trailed his fingers up and down her back.

"Five," she blurted.

"Five what?"

"I've slept with five guys." Holly angled to look in his eyes. "Including you."

Nick kept his surprise in check. His cop side searched her eyes and her face for the lie. Finding none, a purely primitive male instinct of *mine mine mine* rolled through him. He reconnected their mouths in a kiss so tender he felt her satisfied sigh slip into his soul.

Suddenly she stiffened and broke free when his tongue swept between her lips. "Oh, you probably wish I would get a drink first—"

"No." He sucked on her tongue before releasing it. "I wanna know how my come tastes in your mouth." Then Nick swamped her with kisses that caused her to writhe against him. Kisses that plainly said she wanted him again as much as he wanted her.

This time Nick backed away first and rested his forehead to hers. "Again, Holly. Like this. Wrapped tightly together, looking in each other's eyes, slipping and sliding as we're making love in a cocoon of water."

She scattered kisses over his jawline to his ear. "But all the condoms are in the bedroom."

"Damn. Then I guess I'll have you all slippery and wet in bed." He helped her stand. His gaze traveled down her long, curvy torso and zeroed in on the droplet trickling from her belly button. He placed his mouth over that shallow dent and sucked the water out.

Holly gasped and goose bumps popped up across her skin.

When she turned, giving him a glimpse of that fabulous ass, he groaned. "I hate to see you go, but I love to watch you leave."

Straddling the tub, she gave a sexy butt wiggle before she spun back around. Her face distorted as she lost her balance, listed sideways, and crashed to the floor.

Chapter Seven

Holly's shoulder smacked into the tile as she hit. Her leg twisted, scraping her knee on the lip of the tub as she tried to keep from doing the splits. Naked. Her arm ended up pinned underneath her body and as she rolled to free it, she whacked her forehead into the metal base of the shower stall.

She squeezed her eyes shut at the immediate burst of pain and the flash of embarrassment.

Oh yeah. Holly North; grace personified.

"Shit!" Water splashed her prone body as she heard Nick hopping out of the tub. "Holly? You all right?"

Good Lord. The last thing she needed was to see his look of pity, so she didn't answer or move.

"Sweet baby, open your eyes for me."

Sweet baby? Her eyes flew open at his new term of endearment. He'd crouched, focusing his gaze on her forehead. "Let's get some ice on that before it swells up more."

Great. It must look hideous if Nick was concerned it could look worse.

He stood and grabbed two bath towels, draping one over her front and one over her back. Before she could protest, he lifted her into his arms.

"Put me down. I can walk."

"Screw that. I like carrying you."

The hard set to his jaw meant arguing was futile. So she kept mum as he strode into the bedroom.

With infinite gentleness, he laid her on the bed. He dried her wet body and tossed the towels on the floor. He propped his hip next to hers and brushed the damp tendrils from her cheek. "Where else are you hurt?" Nick caressed her arm. "Here?"

Holly shook her head.

"What about here?" His fingertips traced every bone in her ribcage.

She shook her head again.

"I can see the scrape on your knee. But do you feel like you twisted either ankle?"

Another head shake.

"Are you hurt anywhere else?"

She nodded.

"Where?"

"My pride," she choked out, failing to hold back the tears. "God. I'm such a klutz. And now I've ruined the whole night." Holly closed her eyes and sobbed.

Nick didn't vanish at the sight of a woman's tears like most men she knew. Rather, he held her hand and repeatedly feathered his thumb over her knuckles, while stroking the sopping wet hair from her face.

Finally she regained control and looked at him. "Sorry."

"Don't be. Accidents happen. If I'd've been on my game, I woulda gotten out of the tub first and then helped you out so you didn't fall." He grinned. "But I was too goddamn busy staring at your ass to be much of a gentleman."

Holly managed a small smile.

"Will you be okay for a minute or so while I get some ice for that bump on your pretty head?"

"Yes. But I suggest you put on a robe or I'll have to beat back all the women who see you naked and will follow you to the room. And I'm not exactly in fighting form."

"Now who's the sweet talker?" After kissing her palm, Nick stood. Robe on, ice bucket in hand, he grabbed the keycard off the nightstand. "Be right back."

"Why don't you just leave the door cracked open so you don't have to mess with the keycard?"

He whirled back around. "Because we're in a strange place and we have no clue about who might be in the room next to us. All it takes is one little slipup, they could slip in and you'd be another statistic."

"But—"

"I've seen it happen in my line of work, Holly, more times than I care to count." Without another word, Nick left and clicked the door shut behind him.

While timing the *throb throb throb* of her pulse, she speculated as to what line of work Nick was in. With his remark about statistics and his earlier paperwork comment, she guessed he did something in the insurance industry. With his abundance of charm, he'd be a helluva salesman.

Holly imagined him rapping on her office door, wearing that dimpled cowboy grin and refusing to take *no* for an answer...as he took her against the filing cabinet. As he took her in the cushiony, adjustable office chair. But her personal favorite? Nick taking her across her desk immediately after he swept everything from the top. Slamming into her as the *ca-chunk ca-chunk* of the calculator spewing miles of tape echoed in the background.

She allowed a secret, smug smile. For once in her life, the reality of a man was so much better than her fantasy.

The lock snicked and the object of her desire slipped back into room. Nick's not-so-quick perusal of her body reminded her she was completely naked. It was unusual she hadn't bothered to cover up in a bout of modesty. Why was it she trusted this man so easily? So quickly? So completely?

Nick headed for the sink and was back with a makeshift icepack. "It's not much, but it's better than nothin'. It should keep the swelling down."

"Thank you." She shivered.

"Cold?"

"Nah. Laying here wet and naked with an ice pack on my head is like cozying up to a fireplace."

He smooched her nose. "Smartypants." Then he crawled beside her, yanked up the bedspread and covered them both.

"Mmm." It amused Holly that Nick invaded her space and was cuddly as a teddy bear, not to mention hot as a furnace.

He wrapped his arm around her waist. "You tired?"

"A little."

"I sense a 'but' coming."

"But don't think my accident will get you out of answering the question."

"What question was that?"

"The same one you forced me to answer. The one where you tell me a tidbit about yourself that no one knows. A secret, remember?"

His groan rumbled against the back of her neck. "I hoped you'd forgotten about that."

"Forgotten? Bub, you're the one who brought it up. So start spilling your guts because we both know you aren't the strong, silent type of cowboy."

"Maybe that's because I'm a lousy cowboy, whether it's the

strong, silent type or the loud, bold type."

"What?" When Holly tried to crank her head around to look at him, he firmly—but gently—returned her face forward and reseated the icepack.

"That's the secret very few people know about me. I'm a terrible cowboy."

"Explain that to this city-slicker."

He snorted. "Most kids born into ranching families know from birth that's the life for them. My McKay cousins are that way. Same goes for my West kin who earn a living from the land and livestock. I, on the other hand, never experienced that feeling of euphoria when faced with backbreaking labor and temperamental animals. Not to mention fighting the Wyoming elements day in, day out. They say what don't kill ya makes you stronger and I realized early on I didn't wanna spend my life half-weak and half-dead."

"So your family doesn't know how you feel?"

"Oh, sure they do. But it isn't like I've come right out and said it, even when I suspect both my brother Blake and my dad always knew the truth. It's not an indictment on their choice, it's just not *my* choice."

Holly adjusted the icepack. "Boy, do I understand that. My sister, Crystal, is happily married to a guy who drives a gas truck. They live in the Jersey suburbs, own his-and-hers SUVs, have two kids, a boy and a girl. Her life revolves around yakking on the phone, watching soap operas, and getting her nails done once a week before she indulges in a four-martini lunch with her girlfriends. My brother, Tim, and his wife just had their first baby. So my siblings and their families have Sunday dinner with my parents every week and they all vacation at the Jersey shore every August. They are close, but that kind of back pocket living terrifies me."

"Does your family know how you feel?"

His fingertips drew tiny circles around her belly button and she withheld a shiver at his surprisingly loving touch. "I guess it's pretty obvious since I rarely go back there. I talk to my folks about once a month. My sister and brother, a couple of times a year. They're not bad people, I just don't have much in common with them any more. I haven't since I finished college and relocated to the Wild West."

"You went to college?"

Dammit. She'd gotten so comfortable with him she'd forgotten she was supposed to be Mistress Christmas, sexual fantasy woman, not Holly North, certified public accountant and certified public klutz. When in doubt, change the subject. "So are you going home to Wyoming for Christmas?"

"No. I have to work the day after. It'd be too much of a hassle with the weather and all."

"Do you have friends you'll be hanging out with?"

"Nah. I'll most likely spend the day at home catching up on sleep or watching movies."

That sounded lonely. It also sounded exactly like how she'd spend her Christmas day. "What kind of movies do you like?"

"Foreign films about the dichotomies of the human condition."

Holly turned and gaped at him. "Really?"

"No. But I'll bet you thought I'd say Westerns, huh?"

She blushed.

"I like comedies. Will Ferrell. Adam Sandler. Ben Stiller. Luke Wilson."

"Me too! *Blades of Glory* cracked me up. My favorite Sandler flick is *Happy Gilmore* and I about fell off the damn couch laughing at *Dodgeball*."

"'If you can dodge a wrench, you can dodge a ball'," he quoted.

They both laughed.

"I wait until I can rent them. Not much fun going to the movies by yourself," she said.

"Tell me about it." Nick nuzzled her cheek and kissed his way to the spot below her ear that drove her wild. "I'd like to take you to a movie sometime. I'd even share my Junior Mints."

"Generous of you," she murmured.

"You'll find I'm a very generous guy." His lips drifted down her neck. "Is your head feeling better?"

She almost said, "What head?" she was so lost in the way he was seducing her with just his mouth. Instead, she answered, "It's still throbbing a little."

"How about if I try to get another part of your body to throb to take your mind off it?"

Her skin prickled with anticipation. "Ah. Yeah. Sure."

Nick swept the pillows to the floor and grabbed the condoms. While he ripped open the package, she ran her tongue over his nipples, amazed by how quickly the tips puckered.

He groaned. "That feels good."

"Tastes good too."

Holly continued to tease him, using her teeth and sucking the flat disks with enough force to leave a mark. She felt the latex-covered cock twitching against her belly and then she was on her back with two hundred pounds of amorous Nick above her.

Even in the dim light she could see his eyes were darkened with desire. "I wanna make love to you, very slowly, and drag it out as long as possible."

"Yes. Me too."

"Let me in."

She eased her knees apart. Then Nick was right there, in the cradle of her thighs, all hot, hard, persistent male. Her pussy was slick, allowing his cock to glide in easily on a single, measured stroke.

"Oh yeah, that's what I'm talkin' about."

Holly canted her hips until that rigid shaft was buried deep enough she felt his balls against her ass.

"Turns me on that you're so wet and ready."

"Turns me on to see heat in your eyes and know it's for me. To know I put it there." Holly slid her palms up the ridges of his pectorals and wreathed her arms around his neck. "Make it last a long time, Nick."

"Be my pleasure."

Nick's kisses and murmured sweet talk demonstrated his need to take it slow. His steady, but leisurely thrusts stoked the fire inside her to the point she feared there'd be nothing left but cinders when he finished making love to her.

He pushed her to the edge, again and again. Finally, when they were both covered with sweat, when they were both struggling for breath, he whispered, "Send us both flying, Holly. Bear down on me." He shoved deep and hard. "Now."

Tilting her hips so his pubic bone rasped her clit, Holly squeezed her interior muscles, gasping as the sensations synchronized and sent her into two shuddering climaxes, one right after the other.

As she fought her way back to the surface of sanity, she was thrilled to realize multiple orgasms were not a myth on par with the red-suited man after all.

"You okay?"

"Mmm. I...my God. That was..."

"For me too, Holly baby, for me too." Nick followed his sweet words with a thorough kiss before he withdrew and left to rid himself of the condom.

Although he wasn't gone long, Holly was drifting off when he crawled back in bed. He put a fresh icepack on her head and his thoughtfulness brought a lump to her throat. This wonderful man deserved better than her deception. She attempted to wiggle away, but Nick held her so closely a sheet of wrapping paper wouldn't have fit between them.

Comfy as she was, her guilt weighed heavier than the blanket covering them. She didn't want to fall asleep in his arms without setting things straight. "Nick?"

"Hmm?"

"We need to talk."

"I know we do, darlin'. But you injured your head and you need to get some shut-eye. I've kept you up too long as it is. And it ain't nothin' that can't keep until morning."

He had a point.

Holly floated in and out of consciousness, never hitting deep sleep. Nick snored in her ear, making rest more elusive. When he loosened his hold on her, she carefully disentangled her limbs from his and sat on the edge of the mattress.

He mumbled, "Not gonna believe I nailed Mistress Christmas."

She froze. Nailed Mistress Christmas. Was that all she was to him? A story he could tell his buddies?

Her empty stomach churned. She'd thought he was different.

He is different. Give him a chance to explain.

Nick might be talking in his sleep, but the truth was, once

95

he heard her confession about not being Mistress Christmas, he'd be pissed off anyway. So maybe she oughta save face and leave him with a memory of one hot winter's night with his fantasy woman.

As quietly as possible, Holly tracked down her clothes and dressed quickly in the near total darkness. When she found the contents of her purse strewn across the carpet where Nick had thrown it, she hastily scooped everything back inside while keeping an eye on Nick, who'd started tossing and turning.

Coat on, shoes on, she gave Nick one last regretful look and set the keycard on the desk before she slipped from the room.

When Nick woke up he had no clue where he was. He squinted at the clock on the unfamiliar dresser. Then his bleary-eyed gaze zoomed to the box of condoms. The empty bottle of champagne.

The empty bed.

Then he remembered. The night of pure sexual decadence.

So where was Holly?

He briefly closed his eyes and let her scent, still lingering on the sheets, engulf him. He let the memories from last night swamp him and fill his body and soul in a way he'd never imagined. Holly was something truly special. He was glad she brought up them needing to talk, because he had a whole lot he wanted to tell her.

Don't you mean a whole lot you have to confess to her?

When several minutes passed and he hadn't heard any sounds drifting from the bathroom, he sat up. What if she'd fallen down? The woman was hot as sin, and yet, he couldn't deny her tendency toward clumsiness, that was somehow...utterly charming.

He yelled, "Holly? Baby? You okay?"

No answer.

A funny, panicked feeling rooted in his gut. Nick raced to the bathroom. Empty. He ran out into the main room and flipped on all the lights. His clothes were in a pile right where he'd left them last night. Hers were nowhere to be found.

His eyes locked on the keycard sitting atop the desk.

Dammit. She'd just snuck out? Without a word to him? Why?

Nick jerked on his jeans, threw on his shirt and pulled on his boots. He found his truck keys in the pocket of his coat. He patted the right back pocket of his jeans and came up empty.

"Oh no. Oh *hell* no."

Frantic, he crawled around on the floor. Looked under the chair, in the couch cushions, under the bed, in the bathroom, on the shelf in the closet, in the dresser drawers and he didn't find it.

He stared at the rumpled bed and then the door and yelled, "Fuck! I don't fucking believe this!"

Mistress Christmas was long gone. And so was his wallet.

Chapter Eight

All morning Holly felt so guilty she couldn't concentrate. She wondered if Nick had gotten mad when he'd woken up and found her gone? Or worse, maybe he'd been relieved? Either way, she'd realized running out had been a childish reaction and she owed him an explanation. For everything.

But her search for his telephone number in the Denver metro area business and residence pages produced no results. True, her own number was unlisted, but that was pretty much standard for a single woman.

What if he'd given her a fake name?

Dammit. Her limited "morning after" experiences left her no choice but to call Ivy, ask her advice and come clean about what'd gone down with one of her club's customers after hours. She touched the receiver. Then slowly took her hand back.

She'd make that call. Right after lunch. All morning she'd been too jittery to eat, but now she was starved.

No. You're stalling.

Holly plopped her purse on her desk. She browsed the take-out menu beside her blotter. Rooting around absentmindedly in the inside pocket for her wallet, her hand brushed unfamiliar, nubby leather. She gasped and yanked her hand back as if it'd connected with a snake.

Heart thumping, she peered inside. Not a snake, but

something made of...snakeskin.

"What the hell?" She lifted out the surprisingly heavy wallet and had a memory flash. Right after she'd arrived at the hotel, Nick had grabbed her purse and tossed it aside. Faced with the sexual heat in his eyes, she really hadn't cared what'd become of her purse or what'd been in it.

Then Nick had taken the first condom out of his wallet and whipped it aside too. Evidently his billfold had landed on top of her assorted purse wreckage, and in her haste to leave, she'd inadvertently shoved his wallet in her purse along with everything else.

Now you know where he lives. Now you can find out if he was who he said he was.

No. That's snooping. That's wrong.

But don't you think he'll want his wallet back?

Yes. She needed a minute to think.

Take your time but you know what you have to do. You know what you want to do.

As the voices warred inside her head, Holly stared at the black snakeskin, as if it really were coiling and hissing for her attention. Taking a deep breath, she flipped the bi-fold wallet open...and froze clear to the marrow of her bones.

"Oh shit. Oh-shit-oh-shit-oh-shit-oh-shit-oh-shit."

Nick West was who he said he was. But the badge on the inside flap of his billfold told her he'd left out one teeny tiny detail: Nick West was a cop.

"Oh shit. Oh-shit-oh-shit-oh-shit-oh-shit-oh-shit."

She reached for the phone.

❖

"This is Detective West," he snapped.

"No offense, but you sound pissed off."

"Newsflash: I am pissed off."

"Like that's news?"

Nick growled. Which only made his brother laugh.

"Is this a bad time?"

"No worse than usual." Nick inhaled and exhaled slowly. "Sorry, Blake, I didn't mean to snap at you."

"I'm used to it, I work with Dad every day, remember?"

"Yeah. Speaking of...why are you calling me at work in the middle of the day? Don't tell me Little Bo Peep has lost your sheep again and you need an ace detective to find them?"

"Fuck off."

He grinned. "That joke never gets old, does it?"

"Says you. If I wanted to be insulted, I'd beg Chet and Remy to keep me company at the Rusty Spur."

Times were tough for ranchers and Blake moonlighted as a bartender at one of the local honky-tonks. "They ain't nearly as entertaining as I am."

"That's true. Especially not lately."

Chet and Remy were the wildest of their West cousins, although tame compared to their McKay relatives. "Why? What've they been doin'?"

"Nothin'. Tryin' to get Colt's house done before more snow flies."

"How is Colt?" Life had thrown the West and McKay families a number of curve balls in the last few years. After their cousin Dag West's unexpected death, their cousin Colt McKay had seen the light and stopped his own spiral toward an early grave. Between Nick, Kade McKay and Colt's younger sister, Keely, they'd found a rehab place in Denver and Colt had been sober for two years. Every day Nick worked with families who hadn't been so lucky.

"Colt's good. Like I said, his new house is almost finished. He'll be livin' up the road from Chassie, Trevor and Edgard."

Nick lifted his eyebrows. His family avoided gossip of cousin Chassie's unconventional new lifestyle with her husband and his best friend. But that wasn't what'd gained his attention. "Colt's moving out of the Boars Nest? Permanently?"

"Guess so. Cam bought both him and Buck out because he wants to live alone." Blake sighed. "I don't blame the man for his bitterness after what happened in Iraq, but he's kinda puttin' his family through the wringer. Cam won't let no one help him. And we've all offered, believe me."

"It's been what? Ten months? Since his injury? He's only been back in Sundance four months. He'll work it out, if the meddling McKays would just back off and give the man room to breathe."

Blake went silent.

"What?"

"Speakin' of meddlin' families...the real reason I'm callin' is Ma wants to know if you're comin' home for Christmas."

Nick sagged back in his chair with familial guilt. "I don't wanna think about anything having to do with the word 'Christmas' today."

When Nick didn't elaborate, Blake drawled, "You gonna explain that to this lowly shepherd?"

With frustration riding him, Nick blurted out how he'd hooked up with Holly. Probably made himself out to be a fool, but hell, it wasn't the first time Blake'd heard about the dumb things his brother had done, and it probably wouldn't be the last.

Blake didn't immediately toss out a smartass remark. Once

again, Nick appreciated his younger brother being even-keeled and not prone to sarcasm.

"You really like this Holly woman, don't you?"

Damn. Blake was intuitive too. "Yeah, I do. That's why it made me crazy this morning when she was gone along with my wallet. If she needed money that damn bad, why didn't she just ask instead of stealing from me?"

"I know you see the shittiest side of humanity on a daily basis, bro, but in this case you need to give Holly the benefit of the doubt. There's gotta be a logical explanation for what happened. For all of it."

A huge weight seemed to roll off Nick's shoulders. "That's what I'm hopin'."

"Besides, you know where she works."

"True."

"Hate to cut this short, but I got sheep bleatin' my name. What should I tell Ma?"

"That I won't be home because I gave up Christmas for Lent."

A soft laugh drifted through the receiver. "Better I tell her that, than you were literally deep in the throes of *Holly-day* festivities last night."

"Funny."

"Good luck. Trust your gut, it ain't failed you yet. And remember it don't gotta be a holiday for you to come back here and visit. I miss your ugly mug."

"Same goes." Still feeling guilty, Nick hung up and looked at the clock. One hundred and eighty-seven minutes until Sugar Plums opened—not that he was counting or anything.

❖

Dishes clattered in the background. As the scents of soy sauce and grease permeated the air, Holly's stomach roiled. She wished she'd chosen a different lunch spot.

After the waiter had taken their order, she leaned across the table. "You haven't said a word since we sat down, Ivy."

"I'm thinking."

"About what you'll do if he arrests me?"

"For what?" Ivy asked. "Ending up with his wallet was an accident. And I know you well enough that I doubt you snooped through his personal effects, besides the accidental peek you got of his badge. Did you?"

Holly stammered, "N-no! I'd never do that."

"See?"

"But what if he arrests me for..." she lowered her voice, "...solicitation?"

Ivy's eyes narrowed, reminding Holly that Ivy had been a top-notch criminal defense attorney previous to her stint as the proprietor of a high-class strip joint. "Did he ask you to give him a lap dance?"

"Yes."

"Did he pay you for it?"

Holly nodded.

"How much?"

"Umm. One hundred dollars."

"Are you serious?"

"Yeah. I-I didn't know what to charge."

Ivy mumbled, "Maybe I oughta put you in charge of pricing, since that's quadruple the standard rate."

"Ivy!"

"Sorry. Dollar signs blinded me for a second. So what did you do after the lap dance ended?"

"Hid—I mean, helped out in the dressing room."

A slight smile curved Ivy's lips. "And Nick returned the night after you performed the lap dance?"

"Yes."

"Did he ask you for another lap dance?"

"Yes, but I refused, because I figured out the one I'd given him hadn't been the norm."

"Then what happened?"

"I left him at the bar and mingled with customers. I changed clothes and Nick was waiting for me in the parking lot when I went out the back door."

"Was that when he asked you to meet him off the premises?"

"Yes."

"At any time besides the lap dance did you ask him for money in exchange for sexual favors?"

"No!"

"At any time besides the lap dance did he offer to pay you for sexual favors?"

Holly shook her head.

"Any and all sexual contact, at every point, was completely consensual?"

Once again Holly's cheeks caught fire when she remembered how eagerly she'd let Nick tie her up. Man. That'd been hot as hell, her powerlessness and his determination to prime her body to reach dizzying new heights, by showing a kinky side of herself she hadn't realized she had.

"Holly?" Ivy prompted.

"Umm. Consensual. All six times."

"Six times?" Ivy repeated, her eyes wide with surprise.

Crap.

"In one night?"

Holly notched her chin higher. "Yes. Six instances of sexual contact and that's all I'm saying."

"And that's saying something." Ivy smirked. "At least you didn't say that's all you were *copping* to."

"Ivy!"

"What? It was funny."

"No, it wasn't. I can't believe this is happening to me. I never ever *ever* do stuff like this."

"I know, sweets, which is why I thought this experience might've lightened you up and you'd embrace—"

"—my seamier, nastier side?" Holly blurted. "It's just made me more paranoid. Now he probably thinks I'm a slut. *You* probably think I'm a slut."

"Because you had a one-night stand, one time? Hardly."

Holly just stared at her.

"Look. I'm the one who should feel guilty for putting you in this position. It's those damn dollar signs that cloud my vision. I shouldn't have asked you."

"*Asked?*"

"Okay, *demanded*, that you fill in as Mistress Christmas. This whole thing could've been avoided—"

"But that's the thing. I don't regret being with him. Nick is the greatest guy I've ever met. Sexy. Thoughtful. Sweet. Funny. Did I mention sexy? I just wish I would've been smart enough to come clean with him as me—the real me—because the other thing I'm afraid of is he'll be disappointed I'm not some wild stripper." A deranged thought flitted though Holly's mind and

105

she laughed. "This whole debacle is like some bad movie of the week, *Accountant Gone Wild*."

"Ooh, I've got a better title," Ivy said, playing along. "*Arresting Behavior*".

"Omigod, Ivy! That's not even..." But Holly erupted into giggles before she could finish the rest of the sentence.

Steaming plates of pork fried rice and eggrolls arrived and they both dug in.

Eventually Ivy said, "He'll track you through Sugar Plums."

"I know."

"Probably tonight."

"I know that too."

"Do you know what you're going to say to him?"

Holly twirled her chopsticks through a puddle of hot mustard. "No clue."

The meal was finished in silence. After the plates were cleared Ivy tried to hand Holly a fortune cookie.

"No thanks."

"Come on. Even if you don't eat the cardboard shell, you have to read your fortune."

"With my luck? Instead of the fortune saying, 'Beware of men bearing Trojan horses' it'll say something like, 'Beware of a man carrying a box of Trojans'."

"Maybe I oughta have you doing standup in the strip club," Ivy said dryly. She cracked open a cookie, fished out the little white paper and slid it across the table. "Read it."

Holly's fingers smoothed out the wrinkles and she read the words to herself.

"Well? What does it say?"

"You will meet a handsome stranger, indulge in the best

sex in the history of mankind...and then he'll cuff you and throw your candy ass in the slammer."

"Give me that." Ivy snatched it and recited, "'Worry not of the past. Fret not for the future. Live in the present; every day is a gift'."

"See?"

"See what?"

"It's total crap."

"Wrong. That's a damn good fortune. And it has that whole Dickensian *A Christmas Carol* vibe going. It's Christmas and Nick is your gift."

Holly rolled her eyes. "What it is, is utter claptrap, hogwash, and horse feathers. You don't really believe in this junk, do you?"

"Yep. Just like I believe in love at first sight, trusting your instincts and second chances, even when some unenlightened folks believe those things are as fictional as Santa."

Couldn't argue with that. "What does yours say?"

"Doesn't matter. It's all claptrap, hogwash and horse feathers, right?" she teased.

"Oh, just quit gloating and read the damn thing."

Ivy crunched on the cookie and held up the tiny scrap of paper. "'Wishes do come true. You just have to believe'."

A strange feeling of déjà vu rippled through her. Hadn't she and Nick talked about wishes? Christmas wishes in particular?

"You look like you've seen a ghost, Holls."

She muttered, "Damn Dickens. This is just coincidence."

"Maybe this one was your fortune."

"No way. I am not putting my faith and pinning my future hopes on the advice from a fortune cookie!"

"There's my practical girl." Ivy gave her an indulgent smile. "Come to the club after work tonight and we'll figure out something logical."

Nick rushed to Sugar Plums after his shift ended. Since he wore his sidearm beneath his topcoat, it was a good thing the overgrown elf wasn't around to frisk him. Still, the lax security at the club made him uneasy.

Truthfully, it felt weird, seeing the place nearly empty. Music pulsed and a rainbow of lights rebounded off the walls, but the stage was devoid of dancers. A few men were hunched at the main bar, staring into highball glasses, ignoring each other. He noticed a couple of bodies bent over the gambling machines in the backroom. The area for lap dances was cordoned off and completely dark.

For the first time in a long time, Nick wasn't sure how to play it. Should he storm through the door warning "No Unauthorized Admittance"? Should he demand to see the manager? Or should he just demand to see the good Mistress?

"Hey, buddy."

His head swiveled toward the gravelly male voice behind the bar. "Yeah?"

"Whatcha want to drink?"

"Arctic Ale."

"Coming right up." The man popped the top on a brown bottle and slid it across the counter. "That'll be ten bucks."

"For one beer? Don't you have happy hour prices?"

The big man shrugged. "Everything is pricey in the entertainment industry."

Nick jerked his chin toward the empty stage. "Don't see any

entertainment goin' on. When's the show start?"

"In an hour."

"Mistress Christmas here tonight?" He took a pull off his beer and hated the anxiety making his head pound.

"Yep." Another customer garnered the bartender's attention and he turned away.

Nick chose a barstool in the corner that allowed him to keep an eye on the door to the backroom and the restrooms, where a mirrored section of the ceiling gave him an unobstructed view of the entrance. Holly wouldn't get past him tonight. No way, no how.

He waited. Sipped his beer. Thirty minutes ticked by. A few more customers trickled in. His cell phone buzzed and he looked at the caller ID. Shit. It was his captain. Nick slid off the stool and headed to the bathroom to take the phone call in private.

Five minutes later he came around the corner and saw her. Mistress Christmas. Long, black leather-clad legs. Red bustier. Bare shoulders. Hair piled on top of her head, revealing the sexy length of her neck.

Nick's pulse throbbed in his temple.

She kept her back to him and was gesturing and laughing with the guy who'd been sitting across from him. Acting as if she didn't have a care in the world. As he stalked closer, he noticed a couple of key things. She must've been wearing stilettos because he wasn't towering over her by a good five inches. She must've been wearing a wig because her hair wasn't a shiny mass of auburn waves, but nearly black.

Finally it was the smattering of freckles across her back that threw him off. Holly had freckles on her nose. His mouth tasted every alluring curve of her shoulder and he hadn't remembered freckles.

Nick tapped her on the shoulder and said, "Holly?"

Unfamiliar cool blue eyes connected with his. "No. Afraid you've got the wrong person."

"Then who are you supposed to be in that getup?" He pointed to her clothes, the exact same outfit Holly had worn, minus the mask.

"I'm Mistress Christmas."

He lowered his voice. "Like hell. Where is she?"

"Where is who?"

"The real Mistress Christmas."

"I *am* the real deal, buddy."

"But—" Nick counted to ten. Where was Holly? He spied the door to the back. "My mistake," he said, then sidestepped her and made a beeline for the private entrance.

"Hey! You can't go back there!"

Once inside the darkened passageway, he zoomed past the dressing area where the strippers readied themselves. A door loomed ahead. Just as he was about to kick it in, Holly emerged.

She stumbled over a fruit basket and tumbled right into his arms. "Nick?"

Frustration set in and he hauled her upright until they were nose-to-nose. "Yes, I'm Nick, but who the hell are you? And where do you get off stealing my wallet and walking out on me?"

Chapter Nine

"I didn't steal your wallet on purpose, Detective."

At her use of his title, he knew guilt flickered in his eyes.

"It ended up on top of my purse and it was so dark when I left—"

"You mean when you snuck out like a thief in the night?"

"I am *not* a thief," she huffed.

"Says you. But I noticed you didn't dispute the fact you snuck out." Nick gave her a quick once-over. "Why aren't you dressed in your Mistress Christmas costume?"

She said nothing.

"I saw the woman out there wearing your clothes. Did you give them to her hoping it'd fool me? Guess what? It didn't work."

"I'm sure nothing gets by ace detective Nick West." Holly reached into her jacket pocket and pulled out Nick's wallet. "Take it. And before you ask, no, I didn't snoop besides seeing your badge. If you hadn't shown up here tonight to claim it, I would've turned it in to the police because I am not a thief."

Nick thumbed through the contents. Satisfied nothing was amiss, he caught her eye again. "I suppose Holly North isn't even your real name?"

"That is my real name."

"Why aren't you working tonight?"

Angry shouts sounded out in the main bar area, followed by the crash of breaking glass. "Dammit." Holly raced down the hallway toward the commotion.

"Wait!" Jesus. Leave it to the woman to run toward potential danger rather than away. He chased after her.

When Holly skidded to a stop he nearly crashed into her.

A man was on his knees with his arms wrapped around the legs of the woman Nick had spoken to earlier. Beer bottles were shattered on either side of him. The man appeared to be sobbing. Or begging. Or both.

"Please. Just one."

The woman was pinned against the wall with no way to escape. "I said no. Let me go."

"Please. Just one. Then I'll go," the man blubbered.

Where the hell were the bouncers?

Nick sidestepped Holly and moved to stand behind the man. "Sir. Release her. Now."

The guy didn't appear to hear.

He really didn't want to pull out his gun, but it looked as if he might have to. "Last warning, sir. Back away from the woman."

"Why should I listen to you?"

"Because I'm a cop."

"Shit." The man cranked his head around. He blinked several times. "Nick?"

Nick's stomach plummeted at seeing his friend's blotchy face. "Rudy?"

Holly said, "You *know* him?"

"Unfortunately."

"B-b-but who—"

He scanned Rudy's disheveled clothes. "Are you drunk? And why in the hell are you on your knees?"

"I'm trying to convince Mistress Christmas to give me a lap dance," he slurred.

Fury surfaced inside Nick at the thought of his drunken friend putting his hands on Holly.

Rudy ignored him and pleaded with the woman, "I have money this time. You can't deny me."

The woman snapped, "Like hell I can't."

"Let her go."

Soon as Rudy loosened his grip, the woman pushed Rudy on his ass and fled behind Nick.

"Stay put. I'll deal with you in a minute," Nick said harshly to Rudy. He faced the woman. "You okay?"

"Yes."

"Do you know him?"

"No, but he's been harassing me for weeks."

"Weeks?"

She nodded. "Claims he's in love with me. The bouncers banned him last month but somehow he snuck in tonight, probably because we're short-handed." She turned and looked at Holly. "Did he harass you when you were filling in for me?"

Holly shook her head. "This is the first time I've seen him."

"Filling in?" Nick repeated.

The woman nodded. "I've been sick as a dog the last couple days and she's been filling in as Mistress Christmas."

His gaze raked over the tall, raven-haired beauty. "*You're* Mistress Christmas?"

Her eyes narrowed. "I sure as shootin' ain't Santa. Who the

hell did you think I was?"

"He thought I was you," Holly said. "As you can see, Nick, I'm not the real Mistress Christmas. And I'm also not even, ah...a stripper."

"Then what are you?"

"I'm an accountant."

Everything clicked into place. Some great detective he made. All the clues had been there, bright as the Northern Lights—Holly's inexperience with lap dances, her discomfort with men drooling over her, the shyness in exposing her body to him. He'd just been so bowled over by how much she made him feel, that he'd ignored the obvious signs.

"So what now?" Holly asked.

"I'll deal with Rudy." He put his lips on her ear and whispered, "Then I'll deal with you. With us. We need to talk about our future, so don't run off."

"I-I don't know what we have to discuss."

"Yes, you do."

"Nick—"

"Please." He inhaled, filling his lungs with the sweet, sugary scent of her. "Just please, darlin'. Don't leave me hanging again."

Her pause seemed too long.

"What?"

"Why are you so anxious to talk to me? Because you're relieved I'm not a stripper? And you think we might actually have a chance at a relationship?"

"We already have a relationship."

Holly's eyes went as wide as dinner plates.

"Besides, I could give a damn what you do for a living. I thought I'd made that clear last night."

114

Finally, she admitted, "I guess you did."

"Good." After a lingering touch to the side of her face, Nick stepped back and stood in front of Rudy. "Get up and start talking."

Holly paced in Ivy's office.

A knock sounded. The door opened. Nick came in and leaned against it, looking weary, but still as sinfully sexy as the first time she'd seen him. Holly asked, "You okay?"

"Not really. I'm feeling all kinds of foolish, if you wanna know the real truth." He briefly squeezed his eyes shut. "Shit. I can't believe I was so stupid."

"About me?"

"About Rudy."

"You sure you aren't a little disappointed I'm not the infamous Mistress Christmas?"

"No. God no. You are everything I've ever..."

"You don't need to keep piling on the flattery, Nick," Holly snapped.

"I'm not. I mean, I am. But in my mind it's not flattery if it's true. Dammit. Just listen to me. Remember when I told you I wasn't a regular at strip clubs?"

She nodded warily.

"Well, that wasn't a lie. Rudy is the reason I came to Sugar Plums in the first place. See, he told me Mistress Christmas had slipped something in his drink after a lap dance, then she stole his wallet and left him to pass out in his car."

"And you thought I was capable of that?"

"Yes. No." Nick scrubbed his hands over his razor-stubbled chin. "I see things a lot worse than that on a daily basis, which

115

is why I decided to check into Rudy's claims off the clock, on my own time. I knew he was embarrassed about what'd happened here, but I hadn't suspected he'd flat-out lied to me.

"I felt sorry for him, which is probably why I believed him without question. His wife left him last year during the holidays. Evidently coming here recreated the memory of happier times."

Holly couldn't imagine how low Rudy must've fallen to believe the limited attentions from a stripper could possibly be considered "happier times". Sadly, she suspected Rudy wasn't the only regular club customer who harbored that delusion.

"Between the lap dances and the gambling machines, it's no wonder he didn't have any money. With his drunken obsession with Mistress Christmas, it's a no brainer he'd been banned, since he's half a step from stalker territory." Nick looked up at her. Intently. "Lucky for him he never put his greedy hands on you."

She swallowed, trying to wet her mouth, which'd gone dry as Aunt Clara's fruitcake.

"Anyway. His choices were detox or jail. He picked detox. Maybe he'll get the professional help he needs since I ended up being such a piss-poor friend."

"His problems aren't your doing," Holly said. "You tried to help him when I suspect the rest of his friends either couldn't or wouldn't."

"Thanks." Those gold-flecked eyes narrowed on her face. "Enough about Rudy. I wanna talk about you."

Holly learned firsthand what people meant when they spoke of a *hard cop* stare. "What about me?"

"How does an accountant end up working in a strip club? Even temporarily?"

"It's not that much of a stretch. Ivy, the owner, is a good

friend as well as a client. I stopped by to drop off some quarterly paperwork and she begged me to fill in. I'd knocked back a couple glasses of spiced wine...and the next thing I knew, I was strutting across stage wearing a bustier, leather hot pants and ankle-breaking heels."

Those shimmering hazel eyes softened. "That first night was the first night you ever...?"

"Got all dolled up, paraded across a stage barely dressed, in front of a roomful of horny men, and pretended to be someone I'm not? Yes."

"Oh baby."

"Then I met you, and followed through with the lap dance fiasco—"

"Not a fiasco. It was the sexiest goddamn thing that'd ever happened to me."

Holly blinked. "It was?"

"Yep."

"But I didn't know what I was doing! And I especially didn't know I wasn't supposed to touch you or let you touch me, let alone have an orgasm with all my clothes on."

A ghost of his sexy smile appeared. "The last time that happened to me, I think I still believed in Santa Claus."

She smiled back at him. "Part of me didn't want you to come back to the strip club, but an even larger part of me wanted to see you again."

Confused, he demanded, "Why?"

"I was afraid a gorgeous guy like you would only be interested in me if I was a wild stripper. Yet, I was afraid if I told you I wasn't Mistress Christmas you wouldn't be interested in me either because you'd think I was boring. Especially if you saw me without all the caked-on makeup and revealing clothing."

"Your *au naturel* look didn't seem to deter me, did it?"

"No. Maybe it was selfish, but I didn't tell you my real identity because I wanted one night with you to be the sexy woman you thought I was. That was my Christmas wish. You just ended up being so much…more than I'd ever dared hope for."

"Sweet darlin'." Nick's voice held bewilderment and something deeper she couldn't decipher.

Embarrassed, she glanced down at her hands. "I never meant to hurt you. Or trick you. Or lift your wallet."

"I understand that now."

"Last night was one hundred percent me in that hotel room. Holly North. Mild-mannered accountant gone wild."

Several excruciating seconds passed before Nick sighed. "Maybe we were both at cross-purposes, at least initially. But everything I told you, everything I did, everything I was last night, was me too. Not Detective Nick West, just Nick West, a lonely man who'd gotten lucky enough to catch the eye and the attention of a beautiful, sweet, smart, sexy woman."

Holly's heart kicked into high gear as she heard his footsteps getting closer. Very gently Nick lifted her chin to meet his gaze.

"Might sound sappy, but the first night you asked what I wanted for Christmas, so earnestly, like you really cared? I almost blurted out the truth."

"Which is?"

"For a long time I've wished for a woman to see the real me. A woman with fire, passion and sweetness, inside the bedroom and out. A woman who could make me laugh, drive me insane with lust, challenge my mind and see beyond my badge, and my redneck background. You are that woman."

"You sure? Not two hours ago you called me a thief."

"Holly—"

"Do you know how bad I freaked out when I discovered I had your wallet? And then I saw that badge? I was half-afraid you'd show up here and bust me for solicitation."

He practically snarled, "Like I said, it wasn't a cop in bed with you last night, it was a man. A man who hopes to see a lot more of you—in bed and out."

"What? You want to...date me?"

"It'll do for now."

"F-for n-now?" she sputtered. "What's that supposed to mean?"

"It means, how we met will be a great Christmas story to tell our kids and grandkids." Nick closed her mouth after it'd dropped open in absolute shock. "Does that surprise you? Or scare you?"

"Both."

"Me too, baby, me too. This all happened so fast. Like some kind of Christmas miracle. Sounds sappy, but it's true."

Tears shimmered in her eyes and hope clogged her throat. "So what now?"

"We build on the magic between us and see where it takes us." He pushed a wayward strand of hair behind her ear. "And maybe I called you a thief because you stole my damn heart, not my wallet."

Holly absolutely melted.

Nick kissed her; his mouth was as warm and sweet as his words. "Spend Christmas with me. We'll do all the traditional things like decorate the tree, bake cookies and snuggle up to watch *A Christmas Story*. Then I'd like to start a few of our own traditions."

Lord, she loved the feel of his lips on her skin. "Like?"

"Like making nekkid carpet angels underneath the Christmas tree. Decorating your body with peppermint-flavored gel. Wrapping you up with velvet ribbon and tyin' you up with garland. I know how it turns you on to be trussed up like a Christmas turkey, darlin'."

Holly couldn't help it; she moaned.

His breath was hot in her ear. "Be my Mistress, Holly, not just for Christmas, but for every day."

"Best proposition I've ever had, Not-So-Saint Nick." She maneuvered him under the mistletoe and sealed the deal with a kiss.

Epilogue

One year later...

"Holly Jolly Christmas" blasted from the alarm clock. Nick rolled over and smacked the plastic box until the cheery song vanished back to the realm of hell from whence it came. He returned to his spot, but the warm, curvy body he'd been cuddled against had moved.

Frowning, he looked across the mattress. Bright green eyes blinked at him, followed by the sultry smile he'd never get tired of waking up to.

"Good morning, Mr. Scowly Face."

"Good morning, Mrs. West." Nick leaned forward and kissed her. "Mmm. I love the sound of that." He stole another kiss just because he could. "Have I mentioned how much I love bein' married to you?"

"We've only been married twelve hours, Nick."

"Best twelve hours of my life, darlin' wife."

Truthfully, the last twelve months had been the best of his life. He and Holly had embarked on a whirlwind relationship. They'd spent Christmas together, were living together by Valentine's Day, and were engaged by Easter.

So at sunset, exactly one year to the day Holly North had strutted across that stage and made all Nick West's wishes— Christmas and otherwise—come true, they'd pledged their lives and love to each other on a secluded Hawaiian beach.

"Let's get up. There's a million things I want to do today besides lay around."

"I'd like to lay in bed and do my wife all day," he muttered.

"Nick!"

"What? Setting the alarm on the first day of our honeymoon is just plain wrong, Holls."

Holly angled over and kissed his cheek, then rolled to the side and stood. Naked. "But I hear they're serving mimosas on the restaurant terrace."

It took Nick's gaze a long time to reach her eyes. His wife was fine. Damn fine. "I'd rather be servicing you on our terrace."

"But, honey, you know how much I love that bubbly stuff."

"Yeah? And just to show you how much I love you, and how eager I am to compromise in this marriage, I'll point out there's a quart of orange juice in the fridge."

Holly's slow, sexy grin appeared. "Then I'll get the champagne."

Miss Firecracker

Dedication

To all those pyros like me, who can't get enough of summer heat and fireworks...

Chapter One

Willow Gregory woke up and realized covering her head with a pillow did not muffle the pounding inside her skull.

She shifted slightly on the damp sheets. The pillow tumbled away and a shaft of sunlight nearly fried her retinas. She squeezed her eyelids shut and muttered, "I'm in hell."

"A hell of your own making," a masculine voice drawled.

Willow shrieked and jackknifed, twisting her body toward the sexy rumbling sound.

Ooh big mistake. Sharp pulses lanced her brain like pointy metal spikes. "Ow. Ow. Ow." She peeled her eyes open, one squinty lid at a time and saw a tempting feast of bronzed male flesh less than two feet away from her.

Holy moly. If her head weren't inside a jackhammer she'd believe she was still in dreamland.

Her gaze moved across the man's thick wrist and ropy, muscled forearm to his ripped biceps, then over the cup of his shoulder to the middle of his chest. His bare, wide, oh-so-lickable chest. His bare, wide, oh-so-lickable chest with an oh-so-delectable tattoo.

She studied the column of his throat, noting the golden stubble dotting his square jaw. Her eyes passed over the dent in his chin and the deep-set dimples bracketing his smirking mouth. She met his gaze. Amused hazel eyes surrounded by sooty lashes were as unforgettable as the rest of him.

Yeah? If he's so unforgettable why don't you know his name?

"Good mornin' sunshine," he said, his voice tinged with a husky twang.

Her lips parted but not a single sound came out.

His smirk became a lethal grin. "How's the head?"

"Like it's got an ax imbedded in it." Willow winced. Ow. Even talking hurt.

"That bad, eh?"

You have no idea. I also have no idea who you are.

He shook his head and the ends of his curly blond hair brushed his collarbones. "There's a reason they call those shots cherry bombs."

"Cherry bombs?" she repeated, immediately regretting the reverberation inside her brain.

"Cinnamon schnapps layered with blue Curaçao and topped with a maraschino cherry. Very patriotic. But that didn't mean you had to drink them all, *Miss Firecracker.*"

She cringed at his use of her former title. "Huh-uh. I handed over my crown, my responsibilities and my title last night." *And good riddance.*

"Your successor might've gotten the crown but, sunshine, you're still wearin' the sash."

Oh crap.

Please tell me I didn't...

Willow's chin fell to her chest. She wore the white satin beauty pageant sash. Nothing else. She yelped, wincing at her own high-pitched squeak as she snatched up the balled sheet in an attempt to cover herself.

"It's a little late for that, doncha think?"

She snapped, "Who are you?" when she really wanted to demand, "How the hell did I end up naked in your bed with the mother of all hangovers?"

"You really don't remember?" he said with a silken purr. "All you did? All you said to me?"

"No. But if you were any good I should—"

He briefly placed his finger over her mouth. "Ah. Ah. Ah. Don't go there. It ain't gonna end well for you."

She paused. Did this fall under the "don't ask, don't tell" heading? She honestly had no experience with this kind of "morning after" situation.

"What?"

"Did it end well for you?" she blurted. "Did we have sex last night?"

"No. But it wasn't for lack of trying on your part."

"*My* part?"

"Uh-huh. I said no. Several times. I might've said yes if I'd seen you strip to nothin' but that sexy sash." He rubbed his meaty hand over his mouth and let his gaze drop to the aforementioned swath of fabric.

Her cheeks flamed.

"But I prefer the woman I bed to be coherent, not babbling about spending a year toeing the line and then demanding I 'man-up' and do my civic duty to help you make up for lost booty time."

Aghast, she whispered, "*I* said that?"

"Yep. After the sheriff left and I got you calmed down."

"Sheriff Mayhew was here?"

"Not up here, but downstairs."

"Downstairs...?"

"In the bar. LeRoy's Tavern. And it's a good thing the sheriff knows your daddy, 'cause otherwise you woulda landed in jail."

A spear of pain shot from her head to the base of her spine and she lowered to the mattress to quell the dizziness. "What did I do last night?"

"Got cherry bombed."

"No kidding."

"What do you remember?" he asked.

"I remember crowning Miranda Sue Maffini the new Miss Firecracker. I remember having a celebratory drink or five with the losing contestants in the back of somebody's pickup. Then we were supposed to meet up here. So I walked from the town hall...then it's sort of blurry." She hesitated. "Was I with anyone else?"

"Not that I recall. You were by yourself the second you strolled in. Didn't seem happy about it either."

A glimmer of memory appeared. Sitting alone in a big booth. Mortified she'd eagerly fallen for the "we'll meet you there" line of crap. Embarrassed and feeling like a loser. Acting like it was no big deal that she'd ordered a round of expensive specialty shots for her new no-show friends.

So she drank them all herself.

The night was a blank after that, which didn't seem like such a bad thing, given the pathetic, friendless state of her life. "I'm in the apartment upstairs from LeRoy's Tavern?"

"Yep." The bed shifted as he scooted up.

Willow lifted her shoulders and studied the guy's all-too-smug, all-too-handsome, all-too-close mug. "So if I'm at Dave's place, where's Dave?"

"On vacation."

"Who are you?"

Two hundred pounds of warm male was right in her face. "My name's Blake West. And who am I?" He swept a chunk of hair from her cheek. "Since I'm managing the bar while Dave's fishing in Jackson Hole, that makes me your new boss."

"I may be hungover, but I'm not stupid. I don't work at LeRoy's Tavern."

He flashed her a dazzling smile. "You do for the next two nights, according to the sheriff."

"What!"

"Might go three nights, depending on how fast you fill up your tip jar."

"What are you talking about?"

"I'm talking about you being a very bad girl last night, Miss—"

"—don't say it: don't even think it," she warned.

"I thought you'd be proud of the title, bein's you're still wearing the sash."

Willow ignored his sexy grin. "That part of my life is over and it doesn't matter. So tell me, Blake West, how bad was I?"

"On a scale of one to ten?" He paused. His golden green eyes twinkled. *Twinkled.* "Fifty."

"I don't believe you."

"The proof is right downstairs. You smashed a barstool into the wall after Norbert Fossum pissed you off. Broke the table too. You did about six hundred dollars damage."

"No way."

"*Way.* And part of the reason the good sheriff didn't toss your cute butt in jail was on the condition you work off the debt, not pay it off."

"Why?"

"Said he wants you to learn a lesson about the high price

129

of, as you phrased it, *cutting loose.*"

Shoot. Willow could imagine herself saying that. In fact, if she thought real hard, she could almost remember shouting it to the rafters after she realized her so-called new friends had stood her up. "And if I refuse?"

"Sheriff Mayhew reinstates the charges of drunk and disorderly, the destruction of private property and you hash out the details in court."

She'd always admired the sheriff's unconventional punishments to keep the peace in their town—until now.

Behind bars or tending bar...was there really a choice?

"Why's he doing this to me?"

"Sunshine, you did this to yourself."

He had a point. "So what are you getting out of this besides free labor? My humiliation?"

"Your humiliation? What about mine?"

"Yours?"

"Yes. You working to pay for damages means I don't have to tell my buddy that I let some smokin' hot beauty queen distract me to the point she wreaked havoc in his bar on my second night in charge."

Silence.

Smokin' hot beauty queen? Wow. Did he really mean her?

His eyes narrowed. "I recognize that scheming look from last night."

"I am not scheming! I don't have a scheming bone in my body."

"Right."

Why wouldn't he doubt her? If everything he'd claimed she'd done last night was true? "It's just...I can't believe I did something so stupid."

130

"Everyone makes mistakes."

"Well, prepare yourself for quite a few more because I've never bartended."

"More used to knockin' 'em back than making them, are you?" he drawled.

Willow glared at him.

Which caused him to smile and set those damn dimples winking again. "No worries. You won't be mixing drinks. You'll be slinging them."

"Awesome."

Blake's gaze trailed down her body. Not a covert glance from beneath his sinfully long lashes, but blatant masculine appraisal. When he deigned to look at her face, his eyes were heated and dark. "Oh yes, indeedy, you certainly are." Then he shoved aside the blanket and stood.

Unlike her, he wasn't naked. However, he looked damn fine clothed. And was there anything sexier than a hunky bare-chested man filling out a pair of hip-hugging jeans to perfection? Her head protested the exertion of imagining Blake West wearing nothing but his dimples.

"...out of hot water."

Willow looked up. "What did you say?"

He smirked, recognizing she'd been ogling him. "I said I figured you'd prefer to go home and get cleaned up."

"Thank you."

"Don't thank me yet. I expect to see you back in the bar in two hours."

"What time is it now?"

"Noon. The bar opens at two."

"How late am I working?"

"Until close."

She groaned. A twelve-hour shift. Chances were good she'd still feel like dog doo-doo twelve hours from now. Chances were even better her new "boss" knew that.

Holding the sheet close, Willow peeked over the edge of the bed. No sign of her clothes. She scanned the floor. Nothing. Ditto for the dresser next to the window.

"Something you need, sunshine?" Blake asked sweetly.

"Umm. Where exactly did you put my clothes?"

He grinned. "*I* didn't put them anywhere. You did."

"This is *not* funny. Where are they?"

"Now, that's the question of the day, ain't it? Look up and to your left."

Willow carefully angled her head skyward. Her red bra and lacy thong dangled from one side of the ceiling fan, her denim skirt and red tank top from the other.

Fantastic. She flopped back on the mattress. Must've been a heckuva strip tease. How was she supposed to retrieve them without jumping on the bed like a naked, drunken monkey?

Thirty seconds later, a soft thump landed on the mattress. Willow turned her head to see her clothes wadded into a ball. "Thanks."

"I'll leave you to get dressed."

"Will I be wearing a uniform today?"

"No. Just a white shirt and jeans. Or a skirt."

At least she wasn't expected to parade around in a Hooters-type get-up.

"Your purse and keys are in the living room. Don't know what you did with your shoes." His eyes narrowed again. "Remember. Be back here in two hours. Or I send the sheriff after you."

Chapter Two

"'Come watch the bar,' he said. 'We never have any problems in Broward, Nebraska. It'll be a cake walk.'" Blake West mimicked his buddy Dave's cajoling tone.

What stuck in Blake's craw about the bizarre events from last night wasn't that he'd allowed the sexy slip of a woman to run roughshod over him, but the misery on her sweet face when she huddled alone knocking back shots. Something about her...called to him. And that was before he'd seen her nekkid.

Blake hefted the case of beer onto the bar top and slammed open the sliding lid on the cooler. The jukebox blared Dwight Yoakam's "Guitars, Cadillacs" and normally he'd be tapping his boot and humming along, but all he could think about was her.

Willow Gregory, a.k.a. Miss Firecracker, had been contrite after the sheriff chastised her. To hear the buzz in the bar, her performance was far from her normal behavior. On the trek to the apartment, she'd repeatedly told him her actions had been above reproach for the last year and she wanted to have fun for a change.

Blake understood needing to cut loose. Hell, last month after loading the last of the sheep, he'd gotten totally shitfaced. He hadn't woken up until noon the next day, which had happened maybe a dozen times in his entire life.

Mornings started damn early in the sheep business. The

sheep didn't care if you'd closed down the bar at three a.m. The sheep didn't care if your head hurt. The sheep didn't care if you had a warm, willing woman in your bed. Sheep needed tending. Period. When you raised sheep your life was dictated by that constant tending. Period.

But you're no longer in the sheep business.

His hand curled around the longneck bottle. For the briefest moment he considered popping the top and chugging the beer. Blake experienced a sense of displacement when he considered the drastic changes in his life during the last four months.

Nightmare words bounced in his brain. Stroke. Disabled. Long-term recovery.

His memory rewound to that day. A normal day. It'd started out the same as always, as Blake and his dad worked side by side in the barn. Then his dad had hit the ground with some kind of seizure.

Luckily, Blake had been right there. Luckily, his dad received medical attention in time. It hadn't been a heart attack like Blake feared, but a stroke. The stroke wasn't as bad as it could've been and the doctor's prognosis had been good. But recovery would take time.

It'd been difficult watching Darren West, his formerly robust father, struggling to relearn how to walk. Directly after his discharge from the regular hospital, the staff placed him in a rehabilitation unit more than one hundred miles from their ranch. Rather than drive two hundred miles round trip every day, his mother had rented a ground level apartment in Casper.

Since Blake and his father were the only ones in their small livestock operation, his father's health crisis meant Blake shouldered all the work, not just half. And half had been plenty before his dad had become incapacitated.

Blake hadn't complained. He just worked himself to the bone and fell into bed exhausted every night.

He'd been grateful to his older brother, Nick, for showing up to help out for a week. But the relief on Nick's face had been apparent when he returned to his wife and life in Colorado. Nick never wanted to raise sheep and he'd bailed out of Wyoming the month he'd turned eighteen.

Oddly enough, Blake didn't hold it against Nick for making that choice. Even when Nick's choice meant Blake didn't have one.

So it'd come as a complete shock when his dad announced he was selling the ranch, the livestock, the house, the barns, the equipment, everything.

Naturally, Blake had bristled. He'd been doing his damndest to keep it all together during his dad's recovery. But his father assured him it wasn't anything Blake had—or hadn't—done that brought about the decision. The bottom line: after two months of rehab he doubted he'd ever be the same man. Workaholic Darren West decided it was time to retire.

Blake's mother was in complete agreement. After living in rural Wyoming her entire married life, she'd developed a taste for living in town. And she preferred quicker access to a hospital if need be. Blake also knew with Nick and his wife Holly expecting their first child, his parents were eager to move closer to Denver. He didn't blame them. He'd miss them, but frankly, the workload had been wearing on Blake for a while.

Then his father shared the most shocking news of all. Their neighbors to the east, who'd been looking to expand, agreed to buy everything but the sheep on the West Ranch outright. The dollar amount his dad named nearly had Blake's eyeballs popping out of his head.

And that was just Blake's half.

The first thing he'd done was pack up his worldly goods from his crappy singlewide trailer and rent a house in Sundance. The second thing he'd done was sleep. The third thing he'd done was become a bum.

Well, not really a bum, although at times he felt like one, lying in bed until eight in the morning. Lifting weights at the community center with his cousins. Playing with his dog. Loafing on the couch with a book until his shift started at the Rusty Spur. Instead of working three jobs, bartending part-time was his sole occupation. No riding the range looking for lost sheep. No last minute handyman projects for his cousin's construction business.

He'd gone from out-of-his-mind busy to bored-out-of-his-skull.

Blake jumped at the chance to manage his good buddy Dave's bar in Nebraska while Dave took a much-needed vacation. Dave was one of the few guys Blake had confided in about his situation after the ranch sale: his restlessness, his worry about his dad, his struggle to figure out what to do with the rest of his life. Bartending in a town where no one knew him would allow Blake to shake the phantom sheep shit off his boots and be someone else for a while.

And maybe Blake could finally fulfill his fantasy of finding a no-strings fling. The women in his hometown preferred his bad boy, hell raisin' McKay cousins to a simple nice guy like him.

Which was another reason he'd sought escape from Wyoming. Once word got out Blake West had money, women who'd never given him the time of day would flock to him like sheep. Another irony, since being a sheepherder had been part of his lack of appeal with the ladies.

Might make him a dreamer, but Blake hoped to find a woman who wanted him for him—even if it was only for a week of hot sex over the Fourth of July. The town was packed to the gills with people attending family and class reunions and the county fair. Surely there was one woman who'd be up for generating some major sparks with him.

Immediately the delectable Willow Gregory appeared in his mind's eye. There was something about the former Miss Firecracker that made him want to blow his Mr. Nice Guy persona straight to hell.

After mopping the floor behind the bar, Blake restocked the liquor shelves. He called the supplier and tripled the beer order. He lined up limes, lemons and oranges for slicing.

He'd just poured himself a Coke on ice when the cowbell on the front door clanked and Willow slunk in. Damn, she looked good. "Feeling better?"

"No. It'll take more than a shower and four aspirin to purge my misdeeds, sad to say." Her gaze zeroed in on his glass. "Are you drinking on the job?"

Rather than ask why Willow had such a low opinion of him right off the bat, he answered, "Nope," very curtly. He pointed his finger at her. "And just so we're straight, no drinking on the job for you either."

"That's not gonna be a problem. Today anyway." She marched around the bar and planted herself in front of him.

Blake looked down at her. The top of her head didn't reach his shoulder. If Mandy hadn't checked her ID he never would've believed she was almost twenty-six. Willow projected sweetness and innocence with her cherubic face, big brown eyes, and wavy chestnut hair. Mercy, he'd like to drag her upstairs and prove that innocence was just a veneer.

"Where am I supposed to put my stuff?"

His gaze reconnected with hers as he tried to forget how perfect she looked naked. In his bed. "There's a locker in the breakroom, which is next to the bathrooms."

"Thanks."

His eyes narrowed when Willow was back in a flash.

"You're scowling at me like I've already done something wrong."

"It's hard to grasp your sudden change of attitude."

She shrugged. "You know the saying, 'When life gives you lemons'. Speaking of..." She pointed to the fruit piled on the bar. "You making juice? Or a fruit basket?"

"Neither." Blake pushed away from the barback. "You'll be slicing them after we go over a few things."

"What things?"

"Learning to take orders, to start." He handed her an old-fashioned waitress order pad and a small round tray. "It might be easiest for you to write down the orders to begin with."

"Write them down for you?"

"No, for yourself. The only time I'll need a paper copy is when you have a big table, ten or more people, and they're all ordering at the same time."

"Got it." She supported the tray on her hip. "Okay, hit me."

"Pardon?"

She gestured impatiently with the pen. "Name some drinks. See if I can keep up."

"Tangueray and tonic. Bud Light. Jack and Coke. Fat Tire. Seven and Seven. Fuzzy Navel. Diet and Captain. Chardonnay."

Willow rattled them back.

"Good. Except for beer. Verify if they're asking for a draft or a bottle." He sipped his Coke. "How are your math skills?"

She offered him a droll stare. "Is this part of my punishment? You're going to make me do story problems?"

Blake laughed. "I hated them in school too. No, I'm talking

simple addition and subtraction. But fast addition and subtraction."

"Can I use a calculator?"

"Nope. You can use your pad if you need to. Ready?"

"For what?"

"To tell me how much the drink order I just gave you costs." He flipped the pad around on the tray. "Here's the price list. Top shelf. Premium. Domestic bottled beer. Imported bottled beer. Tap beer. Wine. Soft drinks aren't listed, but usually those are free for the designated—"

"Forty-one fifty?"

His mouth dropped open. "You figured that out already?" When her stare turned into a challenge, he backtracked. "Wow. You've got a head for numbers." *In addition to being a hot little number that makes my damn head spin.*

Willow reached up and patted his cheek. "And don't you forget it. So what's next?"

"Wiping down the tables. The rags and cleaner are below the sink. I've gotta grab the cash drawer from the office and then I'll help."

He'd only made it a few steps when she said, "Blake. Wait."

He stopped.

"I'm sorry for all the problems I caused last night. For being so touchy this morning."

I wish we'd been a lot touchier this morning.

Blake bit back his retort and listened.

"You probably don't believe me, but I've never done anything like this before. I mean, when I'm mad I yell and get in people's face, but drinking until I pass out? Waking up naked in a strange man's bed? And finding out I performed a strip tease for you—"

He whirled around. "You didn't strip for me."

"I didn't?"

"No. After the sheriff left, you were upset so I took you up to the apartment. I'd planned to drive you home after I locked up the bar. But when I came back a couple hours later, you were naked and snoring on my bed. I slept on the couch. Nothin' happened."

The relief on her face was comical. "I hate that I don't remember. Sounds like I was lucky to end up with you and not someone...less honest."

Blake looked at her thoughtfully.

"What?"

"As long as we're bein' honest? My gentlemanly streak only goes so far and it'd been long gone last night if you *had* stripped for me. No way could I've kept my hands off you. No way. It was damn hard." His gaze swept over her. "It's still damn hard." Boy-howdy was that statement true in more ways than one.

She blinked. "So my behavior didn't repulse you?"

"Far from it. But fair warning. Next time I find you naked in my bed? There's gonna be a whole lot happening. And I guarantee you'll remember every single second of it."

Willow didn't unfreeze until Blake disappeared. Then she sagged against the barstool.

Holy moly. She'd wondered if she'd imagined Mr. Hottie Bartender's attraction to her.

Apparently not.

Blake was the first man she'd been attracted to in a long time—even before her forced abstinence during her reign as Miss Firecracker. She had no clue what to do about the attraction. Men like him didn't usually give her the time of day, let alone the I-wanna-lick-you-up-one-side-and-down-the-other sexy stare.

Forget about it.

Grabbing the bottle of disinfectant spray, she blanked her mind to everything but scrubbing the scum from the tables, when she noticed the chunks out of the wall.

Her stomach clenched. What if she had connected with Norbert's head? She might've killed him. What could he have done or said that'd caused her to swing a barstool at him?

Willow traced the deep gouges and scratches with her fingertips. Evidently she'd held onto the seat portion and the chair's legs connected with the wall. Repeatedly. Luckily she could fix the damage with Sheetrock mud instead of having to cut out the ruined section and install a new piece, which would require taping and lots of sanding.

Blake's footsteps stopped behind her. "It could've been worse."

"Yeah, I could be in jail for attempted murder." Willow faced Blake. Or rather his chest. Her gaze traveled up his broad torso until she met his remarkable eyes.

"Old Norbert hit the ground pretty fast the second you picked up the barstool. So in your defense, I don't think you meant to hurt him, just to scare him."

"Why? Do you have any idea what he said that might've made me act so...rash?"

"Mandy, the cocktail waitress, said Norbert propositioned you."

"Eww! He's older than my dad!"

Blake's mouth hardened. "Dirty old man. Mandy also claimed he grabbed your butt and tried to bury his face in your cleavage."

"That's disgusting."

"Yep. It's also sexual harassment and I don't put up with that crap in my bar. If the sheriff hadn't banned Norbert for his part in last night's events, I would have. So don't you worry about him showing up tonight."

"Good." She swiped the table one final time. "Done."

He whistled. "You're fast."

"Efficient. Now what?" She glanced at the door. "Are we open for business?"

"Yeah. Been slow this time of day. Picks up around four when all the events let out. That's when Mandy comes in."

Willow followed him behind the bar. "So we're alone?"

Blake spun around so fast she smacked her face into his chest. His hands landed on her shoulders to steady her. "You aren't afraid to be alone with me, are you?"

"No. Geez. I woke up naked with you this morning, Blake. I think you've proved yourself trustworthy."

"And here I was hoping you'd try to find my hidden wild streak."

"Do you have one?"

"Everyone has one. I can't wait to see more of yours." He smiled and chucked her under the chin. "Let's finish prep."

He showed her how to load the glass washer behind the bar. Then he demonstrated the best way to slice the fruit for drinks.

Willow stared at him as he dried glasses.

"What?"

"Tell me about yourself, Blake West."

Unease briefly skittered across his face. "Not much to tell. I'm your basic, boring bartender."

"I don't believe it." She let her gaze wander from the mass of curls, down his rugged face, across that solid chest and sculpted abdomen to his lean hips. *Don't look lower.* Yet, she wondered if he was well proportioned everywhere. Withholding a smirk, she met his eyes and pointed the knife at him. "You can do better."

"All right, all right. I'll talk if you quit waving that knife at me and get to work."

"Fine." She turned. *Thwack.* The knife halved a lemon. "Start talking."

Heavy sigh. "I'm a born and bred Wyomingite. I've lived outside of Sundance my whole life."

"Really? I went to Devil's Tower once. Gorgeous country."

"Yes, it is."

"You a cowboy?"

Pause. "Not really."

"How do you know Dave?"

"We went to high school together. He married a woman from here. They ended up divorced and she moved on, but he stayed."

"Are you married?"

"Nope."

"Ever been married?"

"No. I have a dog though."

Willow snorted.

"See? Told ya I'm boring. What goes around comes around. Why don't you fill me in on Willow's world."

Thwack. Another lemon drawn and quartered. "What do you want to know?"

"Your day job. How you got to be a beauty queen."

Willow peeked at him over her shoulder. "The last one surprised you, huh?"

"No. Why would you say that?"

"Because it shocked everyone else in the county." Jerks. *Thwack.*

"I think we've established I'm not like everyone else, Will."

Will. Her nickname. Most men in her employ called her Will, but it sounded different coming from Blake. Almost like a term of endearment.

Wishful thinking.

"But it's fine if you don't want to tell me."

The man was so polite. She turned and rested her behind on the lip of the prep sink. "No, I'll tell you. It's sort of funny in a 'the joke's on me' way. The Miss Firecracker Pageant is always held during the county fair prior to the Fourth of July celebrations.

"Last year, there was a shortage on contestants. So this bitchy girl Destiny, who's been a pain in my rear my whole life, filled out the paperwork in my name and submitted it as a joke. The pageant director, a good friend of mother's, called me two weeks before the pageant, beside herself that I planned to participate as a 'surprise' for my mother. She reminded me to pay my entry fee."

"Jesus. That's cold."

"Yeah. I figured out what'd happened. I was embarrassed, planning to get even with Destiny—after I withdrew from the stupid competition—when my mother showed up at my house. With a beaded evening gown and a boatload of makeup. And hair gunk." Willow focused on a bottle of tequila on the shelf beside Blake rather than his curious eyes. "It's obvious I'm not—nor have I ever been—beauty queen material. I'm like...beyond a tomboy. I skipped my high school prom for a monster truck rally in Omaha. I graduated from Vo-Tech for cripesake. I wear steel-toed boots, not stilettos.

"Growing up I tagged after my dad on jobsites rather than hanging with Mom and learning to cook, sew, shop or do girly things. Clothes, hair, makeup—that whole fussy routine eludes me. In the morning I wash my face, brush my teeth and throw my hair in a ponytail. That's my entire beauty regimen."

"I'm guessing you clean up pretty good, Will."

She shrugged off his compliment, even when it secretly pleased her. "Seeing my mom bursting with excitement about helping me do all the pageant stuff...I couldn't back out. And because people laughed me off, I was even more determined to win."

"And you did."

"Yes, I did. The best part was Destiny's absolute shock. Totally worth parading across the stage in a swimsuit and ankle-breaking heels."

"What about your dad?"

"He was happy about the 'no dating' rule."

"There's a no dating rule?" Blake asked.

"Yep. This is an old-fashioned type of county contest that doesn't feed into any of the larger pageants like Miss Nebraska. It's more...wholesome, so the coordinators expect the winner to be a role model for the young girls in the area. And truthfully, the dating thing wasn't an issue for me, since I haven't dated in forever." Willow frowned. "My dad warned me to expect the guys to razz me about the sash clashing with my toolbelt."

"Toolbelt?" Blake's look was quizzical. "What do you do for a living that requires you to wear a toolbelt?"

"I'm a carpenter."

He grinned. Widely. She couldn't tear her gaze away from

his gorgeous dimples. "What?"

"We have something in common. I've been working off and on as a carpenter for the last few years."

"As a hobby? Between bartending gigs?"

Immediately Blake stiffened up. "A hobby. Yeah. Something like that."

Open mouth insert foot. And the foot appeared to be stuck in her big mouth because no apology poured out.

He tossed his towel on the bartop. "I'll be in the back if you need me." And he was gone.

She hadn't meant for her question to sound bitchy and condescending. Blake hadn't been judgmental toward her at all, when he had every right to be after her bad behavior, so she felt ten times worse.

Buck up, little camper, and apologize.

Five minutes after massacring the remaining fruit, she'd bolstered her nerve to approach him.

Willow tracked Blake to a storage room by the empty box he heaved out the doorway. She poked her head around the corner when she deemed it safe. "Blake?"

"What?"

"I need—"

"Do we have customers?"

"No. But I wanted—"

"If you're done with prep you can start hauling ice."

"Okay. But I wanted to apologize for what I said."

"Nothin' to apologize for." He ripped a cardboard box in half. With his bare hands.

Undeterred by his curt tone, Willow sidestepped the piles and stood next to him. "It came out all wrong. I'm sorry."

"Yeah, me too. Forget it."

"I can't."

"Try."

"But I hate that you think I'm a jerk." She paused. "If it'll even things up, I'll let you say something mean to me."

His look held disbelief.

"No, I'm serious. How about...do they make toolbelts in your itty-bitty size? Or do you shop in the toy department?"

Blake laughed softly.

"Or, I know. Do you need a stepladder to see the drink orders on the bar?"

"Willow. Come on. Stop."

She sidled closer. "I'm trying to be a bigger person—ha ha—and apologize to you. Can't you just accept it?"

"Fine. I accept your apology."

"If I tell you I'm sincerely interested in your background as a carpenter, will you ignore my earlier snotty response?"

He sighed. "Look. I'm between jobs right now and obviously I'm a little touchy about it. So I'd appreciate it if you'd drop it, okay?"

"Okey-dokey."

"Can I get back to work now?"

She didn't budge.

"Will?"

Willow was too busy drooling over his bulging biceps to answer. Without thinking, she reached up and ran her hand from his left shoulder to the bend in his elbow. Yep. Hard as steel. Man. He could probably lift a car.

"What on earth are you doing?"

"I don't know." She ducked under his arm. When she gazed

into his golden eyes, lust punched her in the gut. "Arms like yours oughta be featured in a fitness magazine." Willow touched his right biceps and squeezed. "Ooh, flex for me."

He did.

"Ooh. Do it again." His muscles rippled beneath her palm.

"Now this side. No, do both sides at the same time."

"If I let you feel me up, what are you gonna offer me in return, sunshine?"

Her gaze flicked to him. His face was there. Right there. "What do you want?"

"I'll settle for this." Blake dipped his head and kissed her.

It wasn't a sweet, gentlemanly smooch. It was a no-holds-barred-I-want-you-right-freakin'-now explosion of desire. He shifted his mouth for a better angle, all hot, thrusting tongue contrasting with the smooth glide of his wet lips on hers.

She fell into him with complete abandon.

The way Blake kissed... Man, it felt as if his hands were teasing every inch of her, even when his mouth was the only place their bodies touched.

Blake eased back on the intoxicating kiss, proving his lazy exploration was as potent as his passion.

Willow's head spun. She squeezed his biceps, intending to use his stupendous arms like her personal chin-up bar, when a voice outside the room shouted, "Hello? Is anyone here?"

Blake didn't rip his mouth away and stagger back guiltily. He merely lifted his lips a fraction and whispered, "Just like I figured."

"What?" she whispered back.

"One little taste of you ain't gonna be enough for me."

"Really?"

"Uh-huh. But it'll keep until there's a lock on the door and no chance we'll be interrupted."

Holy moly.

"We'll finish this later." He pushed back and yelled, "Have a seat. I'll be right there."

Footsteps faded. The bell clanked signaling they had more customers.

"You ready for this?"

She stared at his mouth and unconsciously licked her lips. "Umm. No."

"I'm talking about your shift in the bar."

"Oh." She looked at him. "I'm not ready for that either."

Those deep dimples appeared. "Good to know." Blake grabbed a package of bar napkins and ambled out of the storeroom.

It was going to be one very long night. Willow put her hand to her stomach to quell her nerves and realized her hangover was almost completely gone.

Chapter Three

During a brief lull, Mandy leaned next to Willow at the waitress station. "You're not doing too bad for your first time working in a bar."

"Uh. Thanks." Her feet hurt. She'd spent the last three hours running around, trying not to appear as frazzled as she felt. "Are you usually the only cocktail waitress?"

"No. That snot-nosed slacker Ginny called in sick the second Dave left town. She's not sick unless it's from too much sun up at the lake."

"Won't she get fired?"

"No. Dave won't can her lazy ass since she's his third cousin twice-removed or some damn thing. I'm glad you're here helping out, although I'm sure you'd rather be doing something else."

"This isn't bad, actually. It beats roofing in the hundred-degree heat." Willow admitted it was a nice change to work with a woman. Mandy was a riot, quick-witted, sarcastic, not the typical cynical cocktail waitress she'd expected.

"That's right. You run Gregory Construction."

"I run part of it."

"Bet hammering on a roof had nothing on the hammering inside your noggin this morning."

"That's putting it mildly." Willow paused. "So you probably saw the whole thing, huh?"

"Yep. Look, I didn't get a chance to say thank you for going after Norbert with a barstool."

"But I didn't—"

"Do you know how many times he's done that? Stuck his slobbery face in my tits and laughed about it? Knowing I wouldn't do a damn thing?" Mandy chewed her lip. "I have a kid to support and I need this job. But you saw what Norbert did and took action."

"That's not what you told Blake. You said Norbert hit on *me.*"

Mandy's face colored. "I'm not used to anyone standing up for me. I thought telling Blake that Norbert had propositioned you was a better explanation for your umm...aggressive reaction."

Learning the truth about what'd gone down last night alleviated every bit of her guilt about taking a swing at the old pervert. Apparently she retained some semblance of a conscience even when she was drunk.

You know exactly why your conscience popped up and you attempted to pop Norbert.

Every day she dealt with men who held that "women are inferior sex objects" attitude. She'd listened to crude jokes and lewd comments on the jobsite. And if she was a hard-ass to her employees or to her subcontractors about it, then she was called everything from a ballbreaker to a lesbo Nazi.

"Putting up with geezers copping a feel should not be part of the job." Mandy shuddered. "I hope Norbert never comes back. But I'm sure he'll be in his usual spot once Dave returns from vacation."

"Dave never does anything about Norbert?"

"Are you kidding?"

"No, I'm serious because that's sexual harassment."

"I mentioned it several times, but Dave's first priority is his customers." Mandy jerked her chin toward Blake. "I wish Dave would let Blake run the place."

Rather than ask, "Is there a chance he's sticking around?" Willow hedged. "He seems like a good guy."

"He is. He sure went to bat for you last night."

"Pity I don't remember anything."

Mandy cocked her head. "Nothing?"

"Nope."

"I got the impression you two planned on making hot steamy memories the second you were alone upstairs. But then again...since Blake is the Boy Scout type, I'll bet he didn't take advantage when you were wasted, huh?"

"No. He didn't." For the millionth time Willow was glad Blake had been on duty last night. Things could've ended so much worse for her.

"Well, sugar, you're sober tonight." She winked.

The sixtop in the corner waved for Mandy's attention and she sauntered off. Willow heard Blake wiping the bar behind her.

"You doin' okay, Will?"

"Yep. If I haven't said it enough, thanks for looking out for me last night."

"Aw, shoot, ma'am, it weren't nothin'. Just doin' my job. But I wouldn't be opposed to such a purty lady as yourself thankin' me good 'n' proper with a little ol' kiss."

"If I remember correctly...you said you didn't think we could stop at just one little ol' kiss." She peeped at him over her shoulder.

"I hope not. 'Cause I can think of a whole lotta places besides your tempting mouth that I'd love to put my lips."

A fluttery sensation took wing in her belly. Before she could push words past her thick tongue, a customer shouted her name.

For the next few hours, Willow's conversations with Blake involved drink orders. The man defined adept; he could do twenty things at once. Since the place was packed, customers were coming up to order from him, plus Blake had to fill her drink orders and Mandy's drink orders.

He kept up, but Willow was glad a lanky teenage boy showed up to help out. His main job consisted of hauling buckets of ice and dragging trays of dirty glasses back to the industrial dishwasher and bringing clean racks back out.

What bothered Willow more than her cramped toes or the thick clouds of smoke was how few people she recognized in this crowd. She should've known everyone. She was a native of Broward. She was in the prime barhopping years of her life. Heck, up until last night, she'd been Miss Firecracker, the ambassador to the county. Why did she feel like an outsider?

Her attention whipped to Blake. He looked like he belonged here. Smiling and chatting as he poured a pitcher of beer and refilled a bowl of pretzels.

Then Blake seemed to sense her staring at him. Their eyes met and held for a heartbeat or two. No one else would've thought anything of it, but that brief, molten, purely sexual look rocked her to her core.

Maybe he wasn't such a Boy Scout after all.

During a respite, her belly rumbled. She realized she hadn't eaten anything all day besides two slices of toast.

Mandy said, "I heard that belly roar. Blake ordered pizza and sub sandwiches. It's in the breakroom." Mandy snagged

Willow's tray of empty glasses. "Grab something to eat before you pass out. I'll keep an eye on your section."

"Thanks."

Willow skirted the dwindling crowd and fell on the cold food like a starving hyena.

She'd just wiped her mouth when Blake's voice bounced off the concrete walls. "Lord, do I love to see a woman with a healthy appetite."

She took another swig of ginger ale. "Is that your gentlemanly way of telling me I eat like a pig?"

"No. I was talking about all appetites, not just the one pertaining to food."

"Oh." Willow held perfectly still as Blake crowded behind her.

"Although, I'm feeling guilty. I starved you all day and the best I could manage tonight was fast food."

"That's okay. I eat a lot of fast food."

"I don't. I can't stand the stuff." Blake drew his finger down the side of her neck. Goose bumps danced across her skin. "I'm a good cook. I'd like to make you a decent meal after the bar closes."

"You've already done so much—"

"No expectations, Will. Just you and me, sharing a meal."

She slowly turned around. "I'm not usually hungry at two in the morning."

"Then I'll save my culinary delights for breakfast." Blake brushed his mouth over hers. "Stay with me tonight."

"But I..." *Really really want to scream yes.*

"I got the feeling watching you earlier that you were feeling a little displaced."

"Really?"

"Mmm-hmmm. You looked that way last night too, right before you started dropping cherry bombs."

How had he picked up on her melancholy so quickly? Was it true about bartender's intuition? Or was he just that tuned in to her?

"I hate to think of you sitting home alone, stewing about your place in the world and in Broward, Nebraska. And me sitting here alone, worrying about you stewing. Wouldn't it be better for us to be alone together?"

"Then we wouldn't be alone."

"Exactly. And there's always this in the plus column." Blake kissed her. Not hot and hard. Not sweet and warm. His mouth simply...overtook hers. The kiss knocked her sideways, even as he pressed her against the wall to keep her upright.

When he broke free from her mouth, Willow gasped for breath.

He whispered, "You undo me. You have from the second you I saw you."

"Umm. Yeah. Wow. The feeling is mutual."

"Good." His teeth scraped her neck.

"Isn't this against the rules?"

"What I wanna do to you right here in the breakroom could probably get us arrested for indecency."

"No. I mean between a boss and an employee—"

"Neither of us is officially an employee. The 'no fraternizing' rule doesn't apply." Blake retreated. "But I won't push you to be with me if you'd rather say no."

Willow grabbed his shirt. "I don't want to say no. You're so sweet and hot and sexy and nice, but the truth is I don't have a lot of experience with this type of thing."

"What type of thing?"

"Lust."

He grinned.

And just because she'd been dying to, she rose to her tiptoes and dipped her tongue into the deep grooves bracketing his mouth. First the left side, then the right. A sound resembling a growl rumbled from his chest.

She liked the effect she had on him, even when the situation scared her spitless. Willow twined her arms around his neck. "But I feel I oughta give you fair warning. I'm not the wild woman you met last night. I don't want you to be disappointed."

"In what? Your table manners? We're just sharing a meal, remember?"

"Okay. Just sharing a meal sounds great." Once she'd said the words out loud, it seemed less a big deal than she'd made it out to be. She tended to overanalyze everything, preparing for every contingency—real or imagined. Just this once, she wanted to go with the flow.

The bar emptied at one and Blake decided to close early. Mandy and Willow were laughing and trash talking while cleaning up front, which made closing duties fly by. After he walked Mandy out to her car and locked the back door, he saw Willow sitting at the bar counting her tips.

She was so damn cute. Concentration wrinkling her forehead. Her full lips pursed. Her legs swinging back and forth beneath her chair.

He'd worried having her "help" in the bar would actually create more work for him, but Willow had held her own. In fact, even skeptical Mandy mentioned being grateful for Willow's help.

Blake clicked off the neon bar signs and poured himself a fresh Coke. "Want something to drink?"

"Sure, I'll have what you're having."

"One Coca-cola coming right up."

She stopped arranging the dollar bills so they all faced the same way. "I figured you'd have a beer to relax now that you're off the clock."

"Nope. Here's a secret. I avoid alcohol. Working in a bar it'd be too easy to become a drunk. To be honest, I really don't drink much."

"Me neither."

He crunched an ice cube and eyed the pile of cash in front of her. "So? How'd you do?"

"Well, I didn't make as much as Mandy, but she is a professional. After I tipped Deke..." Willow's hand froze. "Shoot, was I supposed to tip out to you too? Is that standard?"

"Depends on the bar. Back home, the waitresses usually give me a cut, even when I get my own tips. Some nights, I make more than they do."

"Did you make tips tonight?"

"Yep."

"How much?"

"You *do* know it's not polite to ask a man how much money he makes, right?"

"How much?" Willow repeated.

Blake angled his head toward her pile. "Ladies first."

She sat up a little straighter. "I made one hundred eighty-two dollars and ninety-three cents."

"That's a nice chunk of change."

"I thought so. Now spill your take."

"Two seventy."

"You made two hundred and seventy dollars?"

"Uh-huh."

Willow lowered her forehead to the bar and sighed. "I'm the lowest breadwinner of everyone. I'm gonna be working here all week to pay off the damages I caused, aren't I?"

"Would that be so bad, Will?"

She lifted her head. "How long are you here?"

"All week."

"Then I guess it wouldn't suck."

"Good to know."

Willow pushed all the money toward his big tip jar. "One hundred eighty-two dollars and ninety-three cents down, four hundred seventeen dollars and seven cents to go."

Blake drained the last of his soda. "You still coming upstairs?"

"You promised me dinner, remember?" She offered him a cheeky smile. "I was going to tip you if the food and the service were impeccable, but since you're more flush with cash than I am...no dice." She hopped off the barstool and impatiently tugged on his sleeve. "Feed me."

"Be my pleasure."

❖

Blake's dick got hard as he watched Willow suck pasta from her fork. Hearing her throaty moan of satisfaction only increased the pressure behind his zipper. "Good?"

"Amazing. Do you whip up stuff like this for yourself all the time?"

"Pretty much. It's easy to cook for one once you get used to it."

"Mmm. I could get *very* used to this type of food." Willow waved her butter knife. "Not that I know the first thing about cooking, even though my mother tried several times to teach me."

"My mom made sure I knew my way around a kitchen before I moved out."

"She's gotta be proud you turned out to be such a great cook."

Thinking of his mom caused Blake a pang. He missed his folks. "I don't cook for her that often."

"You save your expertise for your dates?"

Hmm. She was fishing for information. "The last woman I cooked for was impressed."

Willow's fingers tightened on her fork. "Yeah? What'd she do to show her gratitude?"

"She married my cousin." He laughed at Willow's astonished look. "Indy and I were just friends. I did a little carpentry work in her shop. I only asked her out because my cousin was in love with her and he needed a kick in the butt to admit how he felt to her."

"Did it work?"

"Yep. They threw a gigantic wedding at the community center a month later. Invited the whole town and everyone remotely associated with the McKay and West families."

"Lots of drunken revelry?"

"Nah. Colt and India are both in A.A. But the party at the McKay Ranch after they left on their honeymoon?" He whistled. "Wild."

"Did you get wild?"

"A little. Mostly I poured beer and tried to keep an eye on my cousin Keely McKay, who defined out of control." Blake frowned. "She disappeared for awhile and when she returned, covered in dirt, she was fit to be tied. No clue what happened. She refused to talk about it."

"Are you close to her?"

"Used to be before she went off to school in Denver. I hadn't seen Keely since the wedding, until two weeks ago when Indy and Colt had their first boy. Hudson McKay."

"That was fast."

"Not really. They'd been best friends for years so it was a long time coming."

"So..." She dragged the tines of her fork through the pesto sauce on her plate. "Anyone else you're cooking for on a regular basis back home?"

Blake rested his hand on hers. "No. I wouldn't be here if there were, Willow. I'm not that type of guy. Just because I work in a bar doesn't mean I go home with a different barfly every night."

"I didn't think you did."

"Didn't you?"

Willow shook her head. "I can see where you'd get hit on a lot though. And in my experience—albeit limited experience—guys like you aren't alone for long unless they choose to be."

Guys like you. What the hell was that supposed to mean? Loser, lowlife bartenders? Or because he was big and muscled he had to be dumb and probably fell for any woman who crossed his path? At that moment, Blake was glad he hadn't told her about being a sheep rancher and he was determined to keep the information to himself. "I don't know whether to be flattered or insulted," he said tightly.

"Flattered, definitely." She threw her napkin on the table. "I knew I'd do this all wrong. I didn't mean...heck, the truth is guys like you don't date women like me."

"You know, Willow, that's the second time you've said 'guys like you' so maybe you'd better spell it out, slowly, so *a guy like me* can understand."

Willow pushed her chair back and stood. "Do I really have to gush about how hot you are? How every time I'm around you this funny feeling flutters in my stomach? How I think your dimples are the sexiest thing about you until I look into your amazing eyes? And to top it all off, you're a gentleman and you can cook like a dream and you're so sweet..." Her eyes narrowed at him. "You are way too good to be true, Blake West, so tell me something bad about yourself. Right now."

Blake wasn't supposed to jump her after she rattled off all that flattery? Right. *Refocus.* He snapped his fingers. "I know. I left my dog, Rico, at my cousin's place out in the country because he'd hate being cooped up in an apartment. As I drove away, he flopped on the porch with those big, sad blue eyes like I was abandoning him forever. That's bad."

She stomped over to him. "That's the best 'bad' you can come up with? You care so much about your dog that you sent him for a week of chasing rabbits and squirrels so he wouldn't be stuck above a smoky bar?" She snorted. "I'll bet you are 'bad' to old ladies and little babies too." She whapped him lightly on the arm. "Try again."

Blake yanked her on his lap and pinned her wrists behind her back. "How's this for bad? I really did invite you up here for an innocent dinner. But all I can think about right now is fucking you over and over until you scream my name."

"Really?"

"Scouts honor."

"Hmm. That *is* bad. But I don't believe it." Willow leaned in and brushed her mouth over his. "So why don't you show me how bad you can be and prove me wrong."

Chapter Four

Ask her if she's sure.

No! Slip a condom on and fuck her right here before she changes her mind.

But she's had a hangover all day. Maybe it'd be best if she just got some sleep.

Please. Next you'll be telling me you just want to "hold" her all night.

The devil inside his head even made sarcastic quote marks with his red hands.

The angel just harrumphed.

"Blake?" Willow prompted.

"Hmm?"

"You're arguing with yourself about doing what you think is right and doing what you want, aren't you?"

"Yep."

"How about what I want?"

His gaze snapped to hers. "What do you want?"

"I want you to take me to bed. I want to see your eyes eating me up like they did in the bar. I want to touch you. I want...everything."

He clamped his hands to her butt and stood.

Willow buried her face in his neck. "You smell good. Even after being in a smoky bar all day and slaving over a hot stove, you smell great."

Blake shouldered aside the bedroom door, glad he'd left the lamp on so he didn't have to let her go. He was breathing hard. Not from exertion, from desire.

"You should put me down."

He nuzzled her hair. "I don't wanna put you down."

"But how else are we going to take our clothes off?"

"Good point." He allowed her to slide down his body. He kissed her. Not touching her besides holding her face in his hands. Letting the heat between them build with each kiss. Blake licked and nibbled and sucked at her mouth. When she began to squirm and arch closer, his hands drifted down her neck to the buttons on her blouse.

"Blake."

"Just kiss me, Will. No hurry." He dove in for another hot, wet, consuming kiss.

She produced a protesting noise and ripped her mouth away.

"What?"

"We've been completely honest with each other so far, right?"

Maybe not completely honest.

"Don't take this the wrong way, but I'm not looking for careful seduction. I don't want you to be a gentle lover. Let that naughty voice inside your head win for a change."

"Do you know what you're askin' me?"

"Uh-huh." She lifted to her tiptoes and sank her teeth into his chin. Not hard, but with intent.

His restraint shattered. He grabbed the lapels of her shirt

and yanked. Buttons flew. One flick of his thumb and the front clasp on her bra popped.

Blake angled his head and kissed the hollow of her throat. "I don't care how, but get your clothes out of my way. Now."

Somehow Willow complied.

His hands spanned the width of her trim ribcage and he allowed his thumbs to rub over her nipples until they beaded into tiny points. He bent and suckled. Lapping at the upper and lower curves of her breasts. Loving that everything about her was proportioned perfectly for her petite frame.

He trilled his lips down her stomach and dropped to his knees in front of her.

"Blake."

He unhooked the button on her jeans. They were loose enough that with one quick tug they tumbled to her feet. Blake kissed the soft section of skin between her hipbones. Closing his eyes, he breathed in the dark scent of her arousal as he stripped her panties away. "Spread your legs and brace your hands on the nightstand behind you."

Not a second's hesitation on Willow's part.

He placed a soft kiss on the short, dark curls covering her mound and let his tongue trace her cleft from her pubic bone straight to the sticky wetness between her thighs.

"Oh. Yes."

Blake lost his mind at the honeyed taste of her. He jammed his tongue deep, licking, then plunging and retreating until her legs started to shake.

His tongue zigzagged up that sweet furrow. He settled his mouth over her clit. A few hard-lipped nibbles morphed into solid rhythmic sucking.

Willow flew apart. Making high-pitched keening sounds so

hot and sexy Blake had to squeeze his butt cheeks together to keep from coming right along with her.

Once the pulses quit, he gifted her pussy with one last kiss. Blake stripped. He reached in his duffel bag and snagged the unopened box of condoms.

Her fingers maintained a death grip on the dresser. She kept her eyes on his as he ripped the plastic packaging off the box with his teeth, took out a square packet, tore it open and sheathed himself.

"On the bed, sunshine." Willow paused at the edge of the mattress. He pressed their bodies together, his front to her back, marveling at the feel of her skin, baby soft and slightly damp. He brushed aside her hair to taste the slope of her shoulder.

She shivered.

"On your hands and knees. This is gonna be hard and fast." Even though his balls were aching and his cock straining, he took his time getting her into position. When her body was cradled beneath his, he nibbled on her earlobe. "Ready?"

"Yes. Do it."

But Willow's small build kept Blake from plunging in. Once he was seated balls deep, and slick tightness surrounded his cock, he had to grit his damn teeth not to fuck her with enough force to send her flying into the wall.

"Blake."

"What? Are you okay?"

"I'd be better if you were moving." Willow cranked her head around, challenging him with those liquid brown eyes. "Didn't you say something about hard and fast?"

Keeping his gaze on hers, he pulled all the way out and slammed back in. Twice in rapid succession.

Her lower back arched. Her head fell forward until her hair obscured her face. "Yes. Like that."

He dug his fingers into her hips, mesmerized by the globes of her ass bouncing with each hard thrust as his cock tunneled in and out.

She exploded with another climax that pulsed around his cock, seeming to pull him deeper inside her.

As much as Blake yearned to savor the moment, it'd been an eternity since he'd had sex. The need for release built quickly. Before he could warn her, he came with a hoarse shout.

Once he'd regained his wits, he bussed the back of her head. "Hang tight. Let me get rid of this condom."

Willow mumbled and fell onto her belly. She was in that position when Blake returned.

He crawled on the bed and ran his hand up her spine. "You awake?"

She turned her head. "You completely wore me out."

"You don't want to go another round? Maybe it'd reenergize you."

"Tomorrow." She yawned. "I'm tired."

He caressed her sweet curves. "You want one of my shirts to sleep in?"

"I thought that big, hot body of yours could keep me warm."

"Sounds good." Blake switched off the lamp. He scooted in behind her and she immediately snuggled into his chest.

"I forgot to tell you thanks for dinner." She kissed his pectoral. "And thanks for the outstanding orgasm."

"More where that came from. Get some sleep. We have another long day tomorrow." And if he had his way, a very long morning spent between the sheets and her thighs before they even made it downstairs.

❖

Willow was cold. She rolled, hoping to reconnect with Blake's body heat, but he wasn't there.

She blinked and saw him lounging against the wall, staring at her. She smiled sleepily. "Hey."

"That's much better than the shriek I got yesterday morning."

"That's because I'm not surprised to see you today."

"But you're happy to see me?"

"Very."

"Good. Because I've been waiting for you to wake up so I can give you a proper good mornin' kiss."

"Can I brush my teeth first?"

He grinned. "Oh, it ain't your mouth I plan on kissing."

Bye-bye sleepy; hello wide-awake.

"Spread your legs."

She didn't utter a peep of protest. As long as he put his mouth on her he could command her all day as far as she was concerned. Willow kicked the covers away.

"Wider."

She let her right heel touch the edge of the bed and slid her left heel until it nearly touched the wall.

"Scoot up."

Willow propped herself up on her elbows to watch Blake shimmy on his belly between her thighs. "I think your shoulders are almost as wide as the bed."

"Flattery will get you everywhere with me."

"Handy, then, isn't it, that you're exactly where I want you to be?"

"Mmm-hmm."

Then he began to work her over with his mouth. Suckling kisses and nibbles interspersed with long, wet licks of his tongue. He spread her pussy lips apart with his thumbs and sucked directly on her clit until she was primed to blow and then he backed off. Next he tickled her skin with the ends of his hair as he rubbed his open mouth up and down the tops of her thighs.

But it wasn't torture, it was...humbling, Blake's undivided attention to her pleasure. Figuring out what she liked. What made her giggle. Or what made her beg.

Oh and she begged. Repeatedly.

The first time he brought her to orgasm just by using the barest flick of his tongue across her clit. She hadn't caught her breath and Blake started in again. He scattered kisses up the inside of her thighs.

The second time he brought her to orgasm with two fingers pumping in and out of her wet pussy as he suckled her clit. She'd gripped his head and ground her sex against his face. Blake's possessive growling noise set her off as fast and loud as a Black Cat firecracker.

Willow flopped back on the mattress and briefly contemplated crossing her legs to give herself time to recover. But Blake would see that as a challenge.

Warm kisses danced across her belly. "Good mornin', sunshine."

"Morning? I thought it was night because that last one seemed to last forever."

"You still haven't screamed my name yet."

169

She snorted. "I could barely remember my own name, let alone yours."

"And yet, I'm not offended by that. Think you can take one more?" he asked and then sucked her right nipple into his mouth.

"Oh. I love that."

"I noticed." Blake peeked at her from beneath lowered lashes. "If you're on top I can suck on you like this as you're riding me."

He looked so earnest, yet afraid she'd say no. Delusional man. "Get a condom."

His dimpled grin could prove to be her downfall.

She perched on the edge of the bed, lusting over the muscles rippling in his butt cheeks as he crossed the room. Man. He had the nicest derrière she'd ever seen up close. Then he turned and she caught her first good look at his front.

Holy moly.

Last night he'd kept his lower half shadowed, denying her the chance to touch him. Blake was such a Boy Scout he'd probably worried she'd be leery of his generous...attributes. It'd become obvious when he'd started working all that hot maleness inside her that he was big. Very big. And whoa—no complaints from her on that front.

She pointed to the condom in his hand. "Are you going to let me put that on?"

He tossed the package to her. "Have at it."

"Get on the bed."

Blake stretched out and his feet nearly dangled off the edge.

Willow had forgotten the steely, yet velvety soft feel of a cock in her palm. And what an outstanding cock. Wow. She could barely wrap her hand around the girth. She squeezed his shaft, sweeping her thumb under the cockhead.

He watched her from beneath hooded eyes.

She ripped the package open and wasted no time rolling on the latex. She placed her knee by his hip and swung her other leg over so she straddled him. "Now you're at my mercy and I can do whatever I want. And I'll start—" she leaned forward and spread her hands across his chest, "—right here. Mmm. You are so beefy. Do you work out a lot?"

"Not much else to do in Sundance, Wyoming," he said dryly. "But yeah, I've been working out more than usual lately."

Willow refused to break the mood by asking about his job situation. Or if working at night freed up his days for time in the gym. "Being muscle bound looks good on you. Very good." Using the tip of her finger, she traced the funky star tattoo on the right side of his chest. "How long have you had this?"

He flexed his pectorals and the star moved. "Not quite a year. It's great isn't it? She's very talented."

She peeked up at him. "She?"

"Remember I told you about my cousin needing a kick in the pants? His wife India owns a tattoo studio in Sundance."

Willow outlined the design with her tongue. Thoroughly.

Blake groaned.

While she ran her hands up and down his biceps, she sucked his nipples. Blake arched into her for more contact.

"Please, Will. Sink down on me. I wanna be inside you." He wrapped a flyaway tendril of her hair around his finger. "Next time you can play as long as you want."

She pushed back on her knees and reached for his erection. Once they were aligned, she lowered slowly.

"That's sexy as sin, watching you take me deep."

"You sure do fill a girl up. Oh yes—" she threw her head back, "—right there. I like this angle."

"Me too." Blake lifted his shoulders off the bed and his mouth latched onto her left nipple.

That extra sensation encouraged her to move faster. She couldn't get enough height to let his cock slide out of her completely.

His hips bumped up as hers slammed down. He switched back and forth between her breasts, alternating little nips of his teeth with suckling kisses. They built a rhythm that left them both gasping. Blake rolled down on his back.

"You all right?"

"I'm great. Almost there." He closed his eyes. "Sorry this isn't lasting long. But you got me all kinds of worked up."

"I like you all kinds of worked up."

"Work me. Squeeze me with your pussy. Like that. Oh, man."

She rested her palms on Blake's pecs, changing the angle so he could pump his hips harder.

"Damn. Here it..." The rest of his sentence was lost on a long, deep moan.

Willow's release was a pulsing counterpoint to Blake's. Sweet. Hot. Perfect. Feeling light-headed, she slumped forward on his chest.

His big, rough hands roamed up and down her back. He seemed content just to touch her and hold her. And she was content to let him.

After a while, Blake murmured, "You asleep?"

"No. But you are a comfy mattress."

"You can sleep on me like this anytime, sunshine."

"I might take you up on that. But for now," she levered

herself upright, "I need to brush my teeth."

"I brought an extra toothbrush. You're welcome to use it."

She smiled. "You really are a Boy Scout, aren't you, Blake West?"

"No. But if it turns you on, I'll take it." He watched as she scooted back and his cock slid out.

"I need to go home and get a change of clothes. Grab my tools so I can fix the dents in the wall. That's part of my rehabilitation, right?"

"Yeah."

Silence.

Ask him to come with you.

No, that'll seem needy.

But shouting his name as you came for the third time...isn't?

"What's goin' on in that clever head of yours?"

Willow sighed. "Look, I don't know if you have anything else planned, or if you want to come with me to my place or not." Part of her didn't want to look just in case Blake wore a polite expression of refusal.

Chicken.

She lifted her head.

And there was that glorious smile. "I'd love to get your tools with you, Willow. But sweet darlin', first you gotta get off mine."

Chapter Five

Blake wasn't surprised Willow drove an enormous Ford Dually F-350 diesel pickup. Although he suspected she'd bought the biggest one as compensation.

The interior left no doubt this was a working truck. Mud covered floormats. Dust coated the dashboard. Papers, food wrappers and empty Styrofoam coffee cups were overflowing between the bucket seats. An extra coat, a pair of coveralls, scuffed boots and a CD case were stuffed behind her seat.

"You don't keep your tools in your toolbox?" Blake asked pointing to the oversized fancy silver toolbox in the truckbed.

"Some of them. But the trowel and Sheetrock mud are in the garage unless I'm helping with drywall."

"Does Gregory Construction do much drywall? Or do you focus in other areas?"

"My end is mostly residential. Dad deals with the commercial side. We stick pretty much to the tri-county area. It's kept us busy in the past, but with the economy in the toilet, it's been slow."

Willow waved at a young woman crossing the street as they stopped at a stoplight.

"What area of carpentry is your specialty?"

"Anything my dad didn't want to do he passed off on me."

He laughed.

"Which means I get the brunt of the remodel work."

"You don't like remodeling?"

"I hated it at first, especially after coming home from a long day and having to live in my own remodel chaos. Now that my house is done, it doesn't bug me so much." Willow shot him a sideways glance. "What about you? What kind of place do you have in Sundance?"

"I'm renting a house. For now."

She chewed on that for a second. "You looking at moving?"

"I don't know. Keeping my options open."

"Your family is there?"

"Lots of extended family around Sundance and Moorcroft. But sometimes it's too much. Everyone and their dog knows everything about you and your entire family, going back generations. It's been a relief to be here where no one knows me."

That sounded ominous, like he was a damn fugitive or something. He backtracked. "As for immediate family, my older brother, Nick, is a police detective in Denver. He and his wife, Holly, are about to make me an uncle." Blake paused. "What about you?"

"Just one younger brother. Jackie. He goes to college in Lincoln. That's where my folks are this weekend."

Easy silence settled between them.

Blake gazed out the window, amazed by the lush, green landscape of western Nebraska, a world of difference from the dry dust and sage of eastern Wyoming. It was flat here, not hilly, with treeless plateaus where you could see for a hundred miles. The humid air was filled with the earthy scent of vegetation.

Willow turned off the highway onto a gravel road. Behind a copse of Cottonwood trees stood an old two-story farmhouse, recently renovated with new Color-loc siding, a new roof, new gutters and high-end Pella windows. The detached three-car garage was new too.

Blake didn't see a barn or another outbuilding. "This place all yours?"

"Yep. I bought it after I graduated from Vo-tech. I couldn't live with my folks, or in town, but I didn't need a place with a large acreage either."

"Not a horse or cattle girl?"

"God no. I cannot fathom spending my life a slave to animals. Only to ship them off for slaughter. Seems barbaric."

Yeah, he was really glad he hadn't told her about his "barbaric" life as a sheep rancher. He'd heard that leading "lambs to slaughter" line enough times and it was another good reason he kept his mouth shut. He glanced across the empty pasture hoping the breeze would cool his flaming cheeks. "What is the acreage?"

"Small. Around ten acres."

"That is pretty tiny."

"Hey, it's not the smallest one around."

"I didn't mean it as an insult. I guess I'm just used to Wyoming 'small' acreages."

"What's considered small there?"

"Anything under a thousand acres."

"Holy moly." She parked on the concrete slab in front of the garage.

Blake hopped out of the truck. She led him through the small covered breezeway between the house and the garage.

A large deck stretched along the backside of the house.

Willow slid a key in the top lock of a set of French doors. She stepped inside and motioned him in. "You want a tour?"

"Sure."

She walked him through the main floor, room by room, detailing the changes and improvements. Blake was impressed with the quality of the work, but also that she'd kept the simple country charm of the farmhouse. Some of the places he'd remodeled with his cousins were just damn gaudy.

"Is the crown molding original?"

"In the living room and dining room." She pointed to the thin, square-cut strip of wood along the ceiling in the kitchen. "Probably overkill to put it in here, but I thought it'd unify all three spaces."

"It looks like it belongs, which is why I asked." Blake smiled at her. "If you tell me you did every bit of this remodel yourself I'll feel like a total slacker."

His comment jarred her for a second, but she recovered quickly. "I did a lot of it myself. Luckily I didn't have many structural changes." She smacked the solid wall with the flat of her hand. "Lots of nights and weekends. Whenever we hit a slow spell and Dad was reluctant to let any of the guys go, knowing business would pick up, we worked over here."

"You and your dad work together on jobsites?"

Willow's eyebrows drew together. "You're the first guy who's asked that. Most guys say, 'Oh, you work for your dad in the office?' because I couldn't possibly know anything about what goes on at a construction site, let alone how to use a hammer.

"In some ways it's been twice as hard being Big Kenny's daughter. New guys think being named his foreman was a gimme. It took six years after I graduated to get the job. If I would've worked for someone else, I'd've had the title sooner."

"But you didn't want to work for anyone else?"

"Nope. My granddad started this company and passed it to my dad. Ever since I was a little girl I dreamed one day it'd be mine. But I also knew Dad wouldn't just hand it over. And proving to the guys who've worked for him for years that I could do it was another challenge."

"How many guys you running?"

"Fourteen. And I'm finally to the point where my crew comes to me first to ask questions, not to my father."

"That's quite an accomplishment."

"Thanks. Umm. You want to see the upstairs?"

"Yep. Especially if your bedroom is up there."

"Figures you'd be interested in that."

Blake was suitably impressed with how she'd combined two smaller bedrooms into one large master. The amount of lace and frills in her bedroom confounded him, especially since he'd seen nothing of a girly nature anywhere else in her house. With the peach and cream color scheme, he could easily believe it was a beauty queen's domain.

Willow sighed. "I need a shower."

"Don't let me stop you from stripping. After all, it is your bedroom."

She wrapped her arms around one of the wooden posts on the bed and studied him.

"What?"

"I don't know how to say this."

"If you want me to leave, Will, just ask."

"No, I want you to shower with me," she blurted.

Well, if that didn't beat all. Blake grinned. "Then it's a lucky thing I remembered to grab a condom."

"Very lucky thing. But then, given your unofficial 'always be prepared' motto, I'm not surprised."

Clothes flew. Willow beat him getting undressed, but not by much. He chased her into the bathroom.

No garden style bathtub for Willow. She entered an enormous glassed-in area that took up half the bathroom. Blake let out a heartfelt moan when he stepped inside the shower. Four sets of jets. Two shower heads.

"You like?"

"Mmm." He peered at the little box below the row of nozzles. "Is that a steam shower button?"

"Yep. I get dirty on the job. My muscles get sore. I wanted this to be a place where I could just let it all melt away."

"You and a couple friends could fit in here."

Willow stared at him for a second.

"What?"

"You're the first person other than me who's been in this shower."

Blake was shocked. Every time he thought he had a bead on Willow, she threw him a curveball.

She turned the jets full on. Hot pulsing spray bombarded him from every angle. As he lingered under the stream of water, he wondered if she could hear him whimpering in sheer bliss. Blake liked nothing better than indulging in a long, hot shower.

Unless it was indulging in a long, hot shower with a hot woman.

Willow scrubbed her hair with some citrusy smelling shampoo. Then she lifted her face to the spray, giving him her back. The white lather slipped across her strong shoulders and down her spine in foamy rivulets, drawing his attention to the curve of her ass and hip. Soon nothing but clear water cascaded across her skin.

He ripped open the condom and rolled it on.

She reached for a razor lying on top of the soapdish. But Blake was too quick. He snatched it up and turned her around. "I'll help you."

Her eyes flashed indecision.

"I'll be careful. I promise. Is it okay if I start at the top and work my way down?"

She nodded.

"Stand like this." Blake pinned her arms above her head with the back of her wrists against the wall. "You look damn sexy like that."

"No tickling me."

"Not to worry. I'll be the picture of restraint while I'm wielding a razor. But after that, sunshine, all bets are off."

He squirted shaving gel on his fingers and worked it into a lather. Then he spread it across each armpit.

Willow flinched slightly.

"Steady."

"I'm trying."

He scraped away the fine, dark hair until the area was smooth on each side and set aside the razor.

Holding her wrists in one hand, he maneuvered Willow under the water. Blake helped her rinse off, leisurely running his free hand down the inside of her arm, past her armpit and over her breast. He reversed the motion until each pass became a constant caress from her wrist to her ribcage.

He loved the way she moaned and leaned against him. He really loved her feminine gasp when she felt his rigid cock pressing into her back.

Blake switched hands and gave Willow the same thorough treatment on her other side. By the time he finished she was shaking.

"Cold?" he murmured, licking droplets of water from the skin below her ear.

"No."

"Good. 'Cause I still have to do your legs."

"I just shaved them yesterday so they don't need it." Willow looked at him over her shoulder. "Blake?"

"Hmm?"

"Are we done playing water torture games? Because I'd sure like you to fuck me."

He froze. "Willow Gregory! I think that's the first time I've heard you cuss."

"That's because I don't cuss."

"Working in the construction biz and around foul-mouthed welders and you don't swear?"

"Huh-uh. Early on, my mom was afraid I'd end up with a mouth like my father's, so she made him fine me every time I uttered anything close to a swear word. I lost the habit fairly quickly." Her eyes narrowed. "However, I swear if you don't fuck me right now, I will cuss and scream and throw a tantrum like you've never seen."

Blake let go of her arms. He stepped in front of her, crushed his mouth to hers even as he hoisted her up against the tiled wall. His dick was in perfect position and he slid into her pussy in one long glide.

They moaned in unison.

She was wet. Inside. Outside. She was soft. Inside. Outside.

As he began to thrust, her thighs gripped his hips. Her fingers were in his hair, urging him to keep kissing her. The *slap slap slap* of their skin echoed as thick ribbons of steam wrapped around them like hot silk.

Blake wanted to take his time making love to her. So he

did. Pushing them higher. Slowly. Steadily. Until that moment they both needed more. Harder, faster deeper.

Her pussy clenched tightly around his cock, milking his orgasm with the strength of hers. They held to each other as they spiraled over the edge of pleasure together.

His legs and his arms shook like he'd run a marathon. Had Willow felt that same connection? Or would she think that shower sex was always that intense?

Her breath tickled his ear. "Put me down."

"I don't wanna."

"You're going to get a cramp, and then you'll drop me, and I'll break my wrist or something stupid and you'll feel all guilty, so—"

"Okay, okay." Blake pecked her on the lips and set her on her feet. He turned all the jets off and it was suddenly very quiet.

Willow wrapped her arms around him from behind. "Thank you for helping me christen my shower, Blake."

"My pleasure." Would she invite other men into her shower now that he'd helped her break it in?

Probably.

Why did he feel so damn jealous?

Because you aren't a no-strings kind of guy. And she's the type of woman you want to tie to you forever.

Twenty minutes later Willow was tossing a small bucket of wall-patching supplies into her truck bed when a familiar pickup started up the drive.

Her gaze zoomed to Blake. His hair was still damp and he had that sated look men got after sex. The fact he wore it after having sex with her made her want to cheer. The fact that Paul, the electrician and the company's biggest gossip, would also see that look on Blake, made her want to hide in the garage.

You're a big girl. Not a Daddy's girl. You're entitled to put a big ol' she-rocked-my-world smile on any man's face.

Paul parked his rig next to hers but didn't bother to get out. "Hey, Will."

"Hey, Paul. What's up?"

"I haven't seen you around for a day or so. When I saw your truck out here, I thought I'd check and see if everything is okay, bein's your dad is out of town."

"Everything's fine."

Paul's gaze flickered between Willow and Blake.

She could see Paul sizing up the situation and her first thought was to run interference. "Paul, this is Blake West. Blake, Paul Shulman."

Blake walked over so he could shake Paul's hand through the pickup window. "Nice to meetcha, Paul."

"Same goes. So, Blake. What brings you to Broward?"

"Blake is filling in for Dave at LeRoy's Tavern."

Blake sent her a why-are-you-speaking-for-me look.

"A bartender, huh?"

"Yep."

"You planning to stick around these parts? Or is this temporary?"

Blake said, "It depends," at the same time Willow said, "Temporary."

"He's headed back to Sundance when Dave returns," Willow said in a rush. Shoot. She'd done it again.

"You tend bar in Wyoming?"

"Yeah." Blake's eyes shot daggers at Willow daring her to

contradict him.

"Whereabouts in Wyoming?"

"Sundance."

"Beautiful country. I suppose there's always a need for bartenders."

Blake shrugged. "There are worse things."

Paul pointed to the open tailgate and the buckets in Willow's truck bed. "Whatcha got there?"

"Oh nothing." She slammed the tailgate shut, hoping to hide her overnight bag from Paul's prying eyes. "Just a fix-up I'm doing at LeRoy's to help Blake out. No big deal."

But by the way Paul's eyes narrowed, it'd become a big deal. "Since when do you hang out at LeRoy's?"

Was she supposed to confess she'd gone on a drunken rampage she didn't remember and trashed the place? Before Willow considered the implications, she looked at Blake instead of answering. When she realized what she'd done, it was too late.

Paul smiled, which scared Willow far worse than Paul's scheming expression. "I won't keep you from exercising your helpful nature, Will. When did your dad say he'd be back?"

That big jerk. Paul knew *exactly* when her father planned to return. "Tuesday."

"Yeah, I believe you're right." He nodded at Blake. "Good meeting you. Take care. You need anything, holler."

"Thanks."

She didn't say a word until Paul's truck was gone.

"Interesting friend you have there," Blake said. He shoved her duffel bag beneath the toolbox.

"He's not my friend; he's my employee."

"At any rate, word's gonna get around town about you bein'

out with me."

"Does that bother you?"

"No." He paused. "But I'm pretty sure it bothers you."

Before she could protest, he'd climbed into the truck and slammed the door.

Halfway into town, Willow decided enough with the silence. "Look, Blake—"

"No need to explain. In fact, I wish you wouldn't." He directed his sigh out the window. "I understand. And believe it or not, I'm used to it."

Darn it. She didn't want his easy acceptance. She wanted his anger. Maybe even a hint of his possessiveness. She wanted to know where she stood with him.

With the standoffish way he's acting, you already know.

Willow just didn't know what to do about it.

❖

Another slow afternoon in the bar business.

She and Blake hadn't spoken much. If he wasn't busy restocking or handling phone calls, he was in the office doing paperwork.

Right. He was avoiding her.

Do you blame him?

No. But this was the perfect example of why she hadn't had a steady boyfriend since she'd been away at Vo-tech. This male/female sex thing seemed harder as she got older, not easier.

She spent her days surrounded by men, but she couldn't get a date to save her life. Even if it weren't against company

185

rules for her to "fraternize" with the men who worked for her, Willow doubted they'd be lining up to ask her out anyway.

First of all, any potential date would have to deal with her father.

Second of all, very few of the men she knew actually saw her as a woman. She was "Will", their buddy, their pal, their boss.

Maybe that was another reason she hadn't skipped out when Destiny had tossed her name in the Miss Firecracker ring. If guys around here heard she'd been in the running for the coveted title of "beauty queen" some man would buck up and take her out.

Wrong. She couldn't even land a date after winning the darn swimsuit competition.

How sad: she'd hoped her title and crown would serve as a booty-call.

And oh yeah, Blake West was the ultimate booty-call.

But what did he see in her? He certainly could have his pick of the ladies with that remarkable body, sweet nature and charming smile.

Was she an amusement? Was she just another out-of-town bar booty-call?

The strange thing was, Blake seemed to like her. And he wanted her. They'd had sex three times in twelve hours. Three times. And she'd have sex with him three more times if he asked her.

Yeah, chances were slim that was gonna happen after his assumption she was embarrassed to be seen with him.

Aren't you?

No.

Too bad she couldn't fix things between them as easily as

she fixed the wall. She crouched on the floor and used the trowel to work the mud into the right consistency, comforted by the familiar sound of steel scraping on steel.

Then she applied the Sheetrock mud to the first hole. And the second. The *splat, push, scrape, splat, push, scrape* returned her to the part of herself she'd always felt confident in: her job. It'd probably only take two coats and some light sanding to repair the damage.

She'd just wiped off an excess blob, when she heard Blake's footsteps stop behind her. She felt him studying her handiwork and she fought against bristling up.

Finally, he said, "That looks great, Willow. You definitely know your way around patching." He leaned closer. "Did you use mesh tape to shore it up?"

"Nope. Just mud. It didn't appear to be cracked."

"You gonna do two coats?"

"Yeah. I figure this'll be dry by the time the bar closes and I can put another coat on before I go home tonight."

"What would you charge for a patch job like that?"

"Probably two hundred."

"Then I'll subtract that amount from your damages."

"Even if I'm the one who caused them?"

"Yep."

Was Blake so eager to be rid of her that he'd speed up her repayments?

Can you blame him?

After setting aside her trowel and the trough, she pushed to her feet. When she looked at Blake, he wore the oddest expression. He reached out and gently touched her face. Heat flowed through her.

But he merely wiped her cheek. "Got a little bit of

Sheetrock mud right here."

"Oh. Thanks."

They stared at each other.

"That's not all."

"What?"

Blake let his gaze drop to her lips. "You've got something on your mouth."

Her hand came up as if to wipe it away. "What?"

"Mine." He pulled her close. The kiss was hot and hungry. And public. They were right in front of the windows.

Blake jammed his hands in the back pockets of her jeans and ground the lower half of her body into his.

He was hard. Really hard. Perfectly hard.

The kiss went on and on, from ravenous to sweet back to greedy. When they kissed like this, the world fell away.

Naturally the cowbell above the door clanked, wrecking the moment.

"Geez you two. Get a room."

Blake reluctantly let go of her.

Willow composed herself and faced the customer.

Figured she knew him. Don Dreyfuss, who owned the International Harvester dealership. "Mr. D. What brings you into LeRoy's on this fine afternoon?"

"The missus had to come into town to play Bunko. I thought I'd sneak in for a nip and a peek at the game before I head home." He frowned at the blank TV screen. "What is wrong with you people? Why isn't the Rockies game on?"

"Sorry. I forgot," Blake said. "I had other things on my mind."

Mr. D. sent Blake a sly look. "Well, I can see what kind of

'things' might've been distracting. I don't much blame you."

Blake grinned. "What'll you have?"

"Michelob Ultra. Gotta watch my damn carbs. The wife says I'm getting pudgy."

She let Blake handle the order while she picked up her tools and set them in the storeroom. She'd barely unscrambled her brain when Blake spun her around and pinned her against the wall. "What was that kiss about, Will?"

"Didn't you like it?"

"Of course I liked it. I just don't...get you. One minute you're banging my brains out in your shower. The next you're standing twenty feet away from me practically shouting to your 'employee' that we're just friends. Then you're sucking my tonsils out of my throat in full view of anyone who'd happen to stroll by the bar. So, yeah, I'm a little confused."

Join the club.

"What's going on between us?"

"Do we have to put a name to it, Blake? Can't we just...I don't know, have a good time with each other while you're here?"

"And you're fine with us just havin' a good time?"

It was cute how his cowboy accent became more pronounced when he was angry. "Yes. Aren't you?"

"I'm gonna hafta be, aren't I?"

What was that supposed to mean?

Before she could ask him, he ducked out the door.

Chapter Six

Blake dumped a bucket of ice in the bin, a little harder than necessary.

Dammit. Didn't it just figure?

Can't we just have a good time while you're here?

For the last couple years Blake had been that guy, searching for a good time with a woman who wasn't looking for a permanent relationship. A woman who'd walk away with a smile.

He'd sworn that's what appealed to him, even when he'd never quite found it.

But meeting Willow, the real Willow, not the drunken spitfire but the funny, honest, caring, and capable woman had turned him inside out. She was a woman who wanted to fit in as much as she wanted to set herself apart. She was a woman with spirit and loyalty. She was a woman who was tough as nails, yet as sweet as pie. She was a woman who owned her passionate nature without apology.

Yet, she was also a woman who was looking for a good time. A woman who wasn't looking for a permanent relationship. A woman who'd walk away with a smile.

Didn't it just figure he'd found what he thought he'd wanted...only to realize that wasn't what he wanted at all?

Blake slammed the metal cooler lid and swore again.

Mr. D. blasted him with a stern look over the top of his beer bottle. "Son. That's not helping your situation any."

"What situation would that be, sir?"

"The fact you're nuts about that little gal back there." He lifted a hand, waving off Blake's objection. "Don't bother denying it."

"I'm not."

"That liplock sorta indicated to me she feels the same way about you."

"Maybe she would if she didn't believe I was just Good Time Charlie, the loafing bartender, about to skip outta town when my gig is done."

"Aren't you?"

"No."

"Then don't you think you oughta be telling her that, not me?"

He snorted. "Like it'd matter."

"It might. Then again, it might not." Mr. D. finished his beer and shoved the empty bottle across the bar. "You met her dad yet?"

Blake shook his head.

"You will. If nothin' else, that'll cool your ardor for her right quick. Big Kenny Gregory is an ornery S.O.B., especially when it comes to his baby girl—or should I say, when it comes to men and his baby girl."

"Great."

"Between us?" Mr. D. leaned closer. "It about killed Big Kenny when Willow won the Miss Firecracker contest."

"Why?"

"It proved that rough-around-the-edges Willow was also all woman. And trust me, the men in this town who wouldn't have looked twice at Willow-the-toolbelt-wearing-carpenter? They started paying attention to Willow the beauty queen."

Blake had the oddest urge to growl his displeasure at anyone paying attention to Willow but him. "Funny Willow didn't mention that."

"Can you blame her?"

"I guess not."

Mr. D. tossed a five on the counter and stood. "Good luck, son, because I have a feeling you're gonna need it."

❖

The joint was hopping by the time Mandy clocked in. Willow lagged behind with drink orders. A few of the guys who worked for her decided to come in. They ribbed her endlessly about her new "job" but she wouldn't give them the lowdown. As breezy and sarcastic as her responses were, Blake knew by her jerky, tense movements the situation bothered her.

He wasn't surprised by her curt conduct toward him. Bothered by it, yes, but surprised by it, no. No one in the bar would've guessed they'd spent a good portion of the day naked together. In fact, Blake wondered if he'd dreamt it.

Mandy dropped her tray on the counter. "I need a pitcher of Bud, four cups and four shots of Jack."

"A boilermaker party, huh?"

"How anyone can drink that crap is beyond me." Mandy shuddered. "You a Jack fan?"

"Nope. Hate the stuff."

"Good." She jerked her chin toward Willow's table in the back. "Looks like Willow got herself a fan club."

Blake harrumphed.

"But if the cold stares they're sending your way mean anything...damn, they don't appear to be fans of yours. Did you cut one of them off or something?"

"Not yet."

"Hmm. They jealous you got it goin' on with her?"

When Blake didn't acknowledge her guess, Mandy sighed.

"Look. I'm not blind and neither is anyone else. You two threw sparks off each other from the moment she strolled in here the other night.

"So?"

"So, pretending to ignore her when your eyes follow her everywhere just makes what's going on between you two more obvious."

He leaned in. "FYI, Mandy. *She's* the one who's ignoring me. *She's* the one who doesn't want her male buddies, her employees, to know she's knockin' boots with a lowly bartender."

"Interesting. I don't think the issue is so much that you're a bartender as these guys are surprised that Willow is knocking boots with *any* guy. She's just playing it cool." When Blake placed her order on the tray, Mandy leaned over and rubbed her cleavage into his forearm. She nuzzled his ear, then leisurely kissed his cheek. She pulled back and smirked at him. "That oughta get her hot under the collar."

Blake couldn't help it, he grinned.

Willow spent an hour imagining how crappy Mandy would look bald as a cue ball. After she'd snatched every hair out of the man-stealing woman's head.

As soon as Willow saw randy Mandy disappearing into the back, she followed her.

More like stomped after her.

She found Mandy smoking in the breakroom, her shoulders resting against the wall. She offered Willow a tired smile. "Hey, Will, how's it going?"

"What are you doing?" Willow demanded.

"Taking a break."

"You know that's not what I meant."

Mandy lifted her eyebrows. "Maybe you oughta cue me in since I have no idea what you're talking about."

"I'm talking about you flirting with Blake. Rubbing your boobs on him. Smiling. Whispering stuff. You even kissed him!"

"Does it bother you, sugar?"

Sugar. As if. Willow was about as sweet as vinegar right about now. "Yes, it bothers me! You know that Blake and I are..."

"Are what?"

She gritted her teeth.

"Are you with him?"

Willow glared at her.

"Lemme tell you something. Either you're with him, or you're not. You can't have it both ways. Blake is way too nice a guy to be your dirty little barroom secret."

"Is that right?"

"Yep. And Blake is too good a man to put up with that high school-ish bullshit, Will." She granted Willow a once-over and French inhaled. "If you're not woman enough to stake your claim on him...well, sugar, step aside for those of us who are." Mandy stubbed out her cigarette and sauntered out.

As soon as Willow regained control of her temper, she realized Mandy was absolutely right. She returned out front with renewed purpose. Instead of checking her section, she walked behind the bar and stopped beside Blake.

He had a bottle of gin in one hand and the soda dispenser in the other, mixing the liquids in a lowball glass. "Something you need?" he asked, without looking up.

"Uh. Yeah." She set her hand on his shoulder and rose to her tiptoes, putting her mouth next to his ear. "To say I'm sorry."

Blake turned his head so their mouths were mere inches apart. "For what?"

"For acting like there's nothing going on between us."

"Is there something going on between us, Willow? Besides us havin' a good time and enjoying each other?"

She faltered for a second, but she didn't look away from his mocking eyes. "You know there is."

"Yeah? Then prove it."

"How?"

He shrugged. "You're fast on your feet, remember? You'll come up with something." Then he sidestepped her and reached for a lime, finishing off the gin and tonic.

Shoot. That hadn't gone like she'd planned. Willow felt dismissed. And she didn't like it one bit.

Now you know how he feels.

True. But how was she supposed to prove it to him?

A sultry feminine laugh floated above the bar noise. Willow pinpointed the source: Mandy.

Figured.

Mandy would probably know how to "prove it" to Blake. Maybe Willow ought to storm over there and beg Mandy for help.

Help you to do what? Show you how to seduce the gorgeous hunk you've already slept with three times?

195

Yeah, not the best plan.

Maybe you oughta step aside and let a real woman show you how it's done.

Willow paused. Now there was a great idea. One that didn't reveal her ineptitude. She'd get a crash course in Flirting 101 from Mandy without Mandy knowing. Mandy's tips were twice what Willow's were the previous night, so if anyone had the flirting thing down pat and got the most bang for her buck, it was randy Mandy.

So for the next hour, Willow paid very close attention to Mandy. Her mannerisms. Her habit of tease and retreat. Her loose-hipped stroll. Then Willow tried it out on a couple of unsuspecting customers. And wow. It worked.

Willow zeroed in on her target. Blake. She added an extra swing in her hips, giddy with knowledge that he watched her every movement. Raptly.

She ambled behind the counter. She timed it so when Blake stepped over to fill a glass with ice, she did too, forcing his groin to connect with her backside.

He froze.

Willow peeped at him over her shoulder. "Oh. Hello."

Blake blinked at her. "What are you doin' back here?"

"I needed ice and I didn't want to bother you."

"It'd be no bother."

"That's sweet. Just give me a sec and I'll be out of your way, okay?" Willow bent at the waist and scooped ice from the back of the ice bin, pressing her behind more firmly into his groin.

"Ah, no hurry, Will, take your time." He didn't move. At all.

She jerked upright and pretended to lose her balance. And yep, Blake's big hands landed on her hips and righted her. Just as she'd expected. And he left them there. Just as she'd expected.

"Careful."

"Thanks." Willow cocked her head at him. "Know what this reminds me of?"

"What?"

"Last night. When you were behind me on the bed." She dropped her voice. "That was hot, Blake. I keep thinking about it. And wanting to do it again. And again."

"Willow."

"Sorry." She straightened and pressed her mouth to his. The kiss was more than a simple peck but less than the tongue-tangling variety they'd shared other times today.

Someone from the side yelled, "Can I get some service over here?"

Blake swore under his breath and released her.

Willow returned to her section, mighty pleased.

Next, she "accidentally" spilled ice water on herself, forcing Blake to see her mopping water from her chest and picking ice cubes out of her cleavage. And he did watch. With those hooded eyes, causing her body to tighten in all the right places.

Her blatant pursuit took a toll on him. So when Willow saw Blake rubbing the back of his neck, she felt guilty. "Want me to do that?"

"No, it's okay—" was all he eked out before she plunked him on the barstool behind the bar.

Amidst his half-hearted protests, she dug her thumbs into his shoulder blades. "This'd be easier if you didn't have a shirt on." She rubbed the tight bulges, imagining her tongue tracing the defined muscles. Tasting the salt on his skin. "You'd probably rake in the tips too."

He snorted.

She massaged the knobs of his spine from the base to his hairline. "If I had more time, I'd loosen every bit of tension." She buried her nose in his hair, whispering, "Isn't that what you want, Blake? For me to ease you? For me to bring you release?"

Blake moaned again.

"You like my hands on you."

"Yes."

She waited a beat then said, "Just think how great my mouth would feel." She squeezed one last time and flounced away to answer a customer's summons.

The rush slowed. This seduction stuff was hard work. Willow needed a breather, but as she bypassed the bar, she sensed Blake's eyes on her.

She'd barely entered the breakroom when one meaty forearm crossed her chest and another banded her hips. His scent wrapped around her and she closed her eyes, breathing him in.

Blake pulled her against his body and started sucking on her neck.

Willow canted her head, allowing him full access to all the good spots, which he remembered in detail. Glorious detail. He used his teeth, his lips and his tongue until she writhed against him. When he traced the shell of her ear and gently bit her earlobe, she gasped.

Blake spun her, fastening his mouth to hers as he pushed her to the wall, pinning her arms above her head.

The way the man kissed was like a drug. Using that velvety tongue until she couldn't think.

He slid his knee between her thighs, creating exquisite pressure by rubbing the thick seam of her jeans directly on her aching sex.

Her moan of approval increased the intensity of his kiss.

She rocked her hips faster, elated and embarrassed one touch from him brought her so close to orgasm. Her panties were soaked. Lost in the urgency, he moved with her, driving her higher.

When Blake broke the kiss and placed his mouth on the sensitive skin below her ear, Willow squeezed his thigh between hers and shot like a bottle rocket.

His low growling sound added fuel to the fire, and Willow could not keep quiet, moaning, gasping, whimpering as her clit throbbed and pulsed as she ground against him.

Blake brought her back to sanity, sweetly nuzzling her cleavage and kissing the skin where her blouse gapped. He released her arms and stepped back.

Willow couldn't meet his gaze: she was afraid she'd say something to break the moment. She rubbed her lips across his pectorals and kissed the hollow of his throat before she retreated.

Their interlude did nothing to cool the heat between them. If anyone noticed the intentional body brushes and extended eye contact they were smart enough not to mention it. Blake couldn't think of anything but touching Willow. Tasting Willow. Fucking Willow.

Time dragged by with agonizing slowness.

Mandy propped her elbows on the bar and sighed. "How can we go through so dang many bar napkins in one night?"

"Because we've gone through a lot of drinks tonight?" Willow suggested.

"You've got a point. I might as well restock them now,

'cause I'll be doin' it in another hour when the bar closes anyway."

Willow offered, "No, I think it's my turn. I'll do it if you'll keep an eye on my section."

"Deal."

Blake took a sip of Coke and waited a full minute before he followed Willow into the storeroom.

She was standing on the bottom ring of the metal shelving unit, trying to reach the package of napkins. She jumped when the door clicked behind him.

He didn't move toward her. He purposely rested against the door because he didn't trust himself not to bend her over the stack of boxes and fuck her until she screamed.

Her fingers curled around the metal shelf. "Blake."

"Willow."

Pause.

"Now that we've established our names—"

She launched herself at him. Her hands in his hair, her mouth hungry on his, her body plastering his to the door.

God. Yes. This is what he'd wanted. What he'd needed. To know she craved him as much as he did her.

Willow kissed a path to his ear. "Tell me you had another Boy Scout moment and stashed a condom in your pocket. Please."

"Dammit. No. We used the one I brought to your place and the rest are upstairs."

"No matter." Her hands attacked his belt buckle. She had him unbuckled, unzipped, and was on her knees tugging his jeans and briefs down before he realized her intentions.

For a split-second, Blake thought about saying she didn't have to do this. That he could wait to get off until they were together upstairs after the bar closed.

But the thought was fleeting at best.

Blake looked down at her. So eager and sexy and... Holy shit she just swallowed as much of him as she could.

It felt so damn fine he could only groan.

Willow's hot mouth and flickering tongue worked him from shaft to balls. No breaks, just constant attention, constant friction. Constant heaven.

The echo of their combined heavy breathing and her sucking sounds kicked him closer to the edge.

Hold off.

No. Be greedy. Been an eternity since you've been blown to heaven and back.

He clenched his hands into fists at his sides, fighting the urge to grab her head and shove his cock deep into her throat.

She pulled off long enough to say, "Don't hold back. I'm not as fragile as you think."

That was all the encouragement Blake needed. He threaded his hands though her hair and held her right where he wanted her. Pumping his hips into that suctioning heat.

Willow didn't balk at his rougher handling.

A humming noise reverberated up his cock, sending goose bumps up his thighs, which started that prickling sensation in his balls. He couldn't tear his gaze away from Willow's face, the splash of color in her cheeks, the perspiration dotting her forehead or the look of concentration that bordered on ecstasy.

She jacked his shaft at the base and focused on suckling the head.

When their eyes met, it was over.

Blake said, "I'm done," as a warning in case she wasn't the swallowing type.

But she was. Her tongue curled around the head of his cock and she sucked in time to each hot spurt. Her constant rhythm prolonged the pulses until he about jumped out of his skin.

He sagged against the door, blinding white spots dancing behind his closed lids. Blood rushed to his head, throbbing in his brain like an echo of his climax.

The *pop hiss* of a can brought him out of his sexual trance. He opened his eyes.

Willow sipped from a can of ginger ale. "Want some? I'll warn ya. It's warm."

"Come here." Blake hauled her upright and smashed his mouth to hers. Sweet soda mixed with the taste of his come and Willow. A potent combination. He kept kissing her until she squeaked a protest.

"Blake."

"What?"

"You're the bartender. People won't miss me but they'll be looking for you."

"They'll be fine for another minute or two."

"It's been ten minutes. You need to fasten your pants and get back out there."

He smoothed a piece of her damp hair behind her ear. "I'd rather stay here with you."

She just gazed at him with those shimmering brown eyes.

"What?"

"So did I prove it?"

Blake grinned. "You even have to ask?"

She smirked. "Just checking."

Chapter Seven

Willow waited a couple of minutes before she headed up front with an armful of napkins. She hoped Mandy hadn't noticed how long she'd been gone. Or noticed Blake had gone missing around the same time. Or that her lips had taken on an extra fullness and shine.

Of course you hope Mandy noticed. Then she'll have no doubt that you're woman enough to handle Blake West.

"Oh, there you are, Willow," Mandy said breezily. "Thanks for grabbing those."

That's not all I grabbed. "No problem."

"Table four needs another round."

"Cool. I'll take care of it." After taking the order, she wandered to the waitress station by the cash register.

Blake offered her the dimpled grin that weakened her knees. "Hey, sunshine."

"Hey. I need two bottles of Coors Light and two Captain and Diet Cokes."

He said, "You got it," but he didn't budge.

She waited. For some odd reason he was fascinated with her mouth.

Hah! You know the "odd reason" he's looking at your mouth.

"Blake?"

"Huh?"

"I'll be back for those drinks."

"Uh. Yeah. Right." He beamed another goofy grin. "Remind me again what they were?"

She repeated the order. She was still smirking a little when Mandy caught her eye and smirked back at her.

"What?"

"Only one thing puts a smile like that on a man's face."

Willow feigned innocence. "Excuse me?"

"Oh, sugar, don't play coy." Mandy pursed her lips and glanced down. "And wow, you've got dirt on your knees."

She blushed, angling her head to look at the front of her pants...and saw nothing. She met Mandy's amused eyes.

"Gotcha." Mandy's smile widened. "And aren't you glad you took the bull by the horn, so to speak?"

Then Willow knew. She laughed out loud. "You sneaky be-yotch. You never had designs on Blake."

"Nope. A little jealousy is a good motivator." She sighed. "I am such a sucker for romance. Too bad I've got none of it in my life."

"No romance? So how did you pick up on the changes between me and Blake so quickly?"

Mandy shrugged. "All in a day's work, but there's no denying you're the *head* waitress tonight." She winked saucily and sauntered off.

The clock slowly ticked toward last call. The place finally emptied out. She and Mandy cleaned the front while Blake wiped down everything behind the bar.

Their section didn't take long, but Blake was still slaving when they finished. Mandy shoved her tips in her purse and waved good-bye to Willow, protesting that Blake didn't have to accompany her out to her car. But Blake was a genuinely good guy who made sure everyone on his watch was safe.

So Willow was surprised to see Mandy scowling as Blake followed her back inside the bar five minutes later.

"What's going on?"

"Stupid piece of shit car. Damn thing won't start. Again."

Blake grabbed his keys. "We'll get it looked at tomorrow. Lemme lock up and I'll drive you home."

"Don't you have to close out the till and stuff? It's already late."

"I'm used to late nights. No biggie."

"I can take you home," Willow offered.

"Will—"

She faced Blake. "It's okay. I'm done."

He crossed over to her and touched her cheek gently, but the fire in his eyes was unmistakable. "You *are* coming back?"

"Do you want me to?"

"Of course."

"Now you have an incentive to finish fast."

"Seems I do. Lock the delivery door behind you when you get back and come find me, all right?"

"Sure."

Outside the air was losing the sultriness. Willow rolled down the window as Mandy climbed in her truck.

"I appreciate this, Willow."

"Least I could do."

"You know, you're nothing like I thought you'd be."

Willow glanced at her. "Same goes. But naturally I'm curious as to what you mean."

"I see you around town and I've always envied your

confidence."

Was Mandy implying she came off cocky? "Yeah?"

"Yeah. But I can't fathom what it'd be like to run a construction company, especially being a woman."

"It has good days and bad days, just like any other job. I'll admit I have a rougher time being taken seriously than my male counterparts. And since I work around men ninety-nine percent of the time, I don't get much chance to indulge in the girly type stuff other women take for granted."

"Is that why you entered the Miss Firecracker pageant?"

Willow shook her head. "This nasty woman I went to school with put my name in as a joke. I had too much pride to back out."

"You won. That had to feel good."

"It did. Doesn't mean I learned a thing about becoming more ladylike, as so many gossips in this town have pointed out to me." *And to my mother.*

"Turn here," Mandy said. "You'd think since I'm on the receiving end of snap judgments I wouldn't do it, but I do too."

Good thing it was dark and Mandy couldn't see the blush stealing across Willow's cheeks. She'd prejudged Mandy. Misjudged her apparently. Yet they were on common ground because Mandy had done the same to her. "What do you mean?"

"Most people in this town think I'm a skanky barmaid biding my time to hook a husband so I can quit slinging drinks. I'm not looking for a man to take care of me. I get by fine and take care of myself. And I am not interested in dating. Especially not guys who hang out in bars."

"Do you like being a cocktail waitress?"

"I'm not qualified to do much else and I am good at it. My

ex split when our baby was six months old. Since he drives truck, and he changes trucking companies like some women change clothes, I don't know where he is most the time so child support is a joke."

"You can get his wages garnished. I've got a couple of guys who work for me who are in that situation."

"I know. By the time they track him down, he's gone again. To be honest, I'm relieved he's not in our life. At least working nights gives me all day to spend with my daughter, Anya."

"How old is Anya?"

"Four. She's the light of my life."

"Who stays with her when you're working?"

"My sister, Roxanne. Our family situation...well, it's not the best. I married the first bozo who came along to escape it and I didn't want the same for my little sister. Roxy moved in with me three years ago when she was twelve so she could go to school here." Mandy pointed at a tiny house set back from the road. "That's it."

Willow parked. "You working tomorrow night?"

"No. Mondays are my day off."

"Oh. Well. Good. Enjoy it."

"Thanks for the ride, Will."

"You're welcome."

"It's been fun getting to know you. Don't be a stranger."

"Umm. Would you like to get a cup of coffee sometime? You and Anya?" She froze. "I mean, Anya wouldn't have to drink coffee. And you could bring Roxy along too if you wanted."

Mandy laughed. "I'd like that. A lot. Take care."

She watched until Mandy disappeared inside the house.

Willow was beginning to think that her stint working at LeRoy's Tavern was one of her better mistakes.

❖

Willow flipped the deadbolts on the back door. Blake wasn't in the office. The overhead lights were off in the main part of the bar and it was spooky with neon glowing across the walls.

"Blake?"

"Back here."

He sat on a barstool in the corner behind the bar. His shoulders rested against the wall and he stared at her hungrily from beneath those super long eyelashes.

"What's going on?" she asked.

Blake held up a chunk of denim and tossed it to her. "Put this on."

She frowned at it. When had Blake grabbed her jean skirt out of her bedroom and hidden it in her duffel bag? The question died on her lips when she looked at him again.

This wasn't the easygoing Blake she'd gotten to know in the past few days. This man was a...predator. A shiver rolled through her but not of fear, of anticipation.

He said, "I'll wait."

Willow had just turned the corner, when she heard him say, "Oh, and another thing. No panties."

Not a request. A command.

Once she'd slipped on the skirt, she realized she didn't have the right shoes. She didn't carry a strappy pair of heels in her work truck. And she didn't particularly want to walk through the bar barefoot. She laced up her steel-toed black boots.

Willow unbuttoned her blouse and tied the shirt ends in a knot below her breasts. After a quick look in the mirror, she released her hair from the ponytail, letting it fall around her shoulders.

She added an extra hip sway as she rounded the corner.

His gaze swept over her. Once. Twice. Then he finally met her eyes. Blake didn't say a word; he merely crooked his finger.

Willow sauntered until she stood directly in front of him.

Blake's knuckles traced the swath of skin exposed between her waistband and where the shirt was tied.

Her belly quivered beneath his teasing touch.

"The boots are sexy. You're the only woman I know who could pull off this look."

"Umm. Thank you."

"You nervous?"

"Uh-huh. I don't know why."

He cocked his head. "Maybe because I'm bein' bossy?"

"Or maybe because you look like you want to eat me alive."

"There is that." Blake smiled slowly as he tugged on the loose knot and the shirt fell open. "Undo your bra, Will."

She popped the front clasp.

Immediately Blake's hands smoothed over her ribcage, pushing the plain white cotton bra and shirt off her shoulders and arms. He bent his head and licked her left nipple.

Oh. That felt so good.

Blake kept licking, lapping the tips, never suckling completely. Nuzzling sweetly, not devouring her like she expected. He kissed his way up her neck to her ear. "You feeling adventurous tonight?"

"What did you have in mind?"

"How about if we switch places and I show you?"

"Okay."

He gripped her arms and stretched to his feet and then plunked her down on the stool.

Willow's face was on level with his crotch. She looked up at him and lifted a brow.

His dimples winked at her. "Oh, I could get used to having your mouth wrapped around my cock a couple times a day, but that'd be selfish. And I'm in a very...*giving* mood tonight, sunshine." He dropped to his knees on the rubber mat in front of her. "Slide down. Put your hands behind you and hold on."

Talk about feeling exposed. Willow gripped the edges of the round seat, which raised her hips higher.

"Now hook your heels around the rungs. Perfect." Keeping his gaze locked on hers, he pushed the skirt up to her hips, baring every inch of her lower half. "Hold on." Keeping his palms on the inside of her knees, Blake lowered his head. He kept his mouth above her sex, close enough his breath tickled the hair on her mound, but not nearly close enough.

Bump your hips so he knows what you want.

Blake knew exactly what she wanted, but he appeared in no hurry to give it to her.

These new power games were exciting. But Willow didn't kid herself about who held all the power right now. Or who was the most excited.

And then that compelling tongue burrowed into her cleft.

She moaned.

He flicked her clit with the barest tip of his tongue then traced the seam down. And up. And down. Teasing swirls. Eventually he wiggled his tongue inside her, curling the end into her slick walls.

"Yes. Oh yes."

Blake nibbled on her clit, then he tongued her deep. But

there was no rhythm, just him tasting, teasing.

Torturing.

Willow's legs started to shake. She was so close... If he'd just stay in one place long enough.

"Patience," he said, then sucked her pussy lips into his mouth.

"Blake."

His answering, "Mmm," vibrated against her swollen tissues.

"Blake!"

He laughed and did it again before he backed off and looked up at her. "Trust me?"

Willow nodded.

His hands left her thighs. "Close your eyes. Keep 'em closed."

She did. He moved but wasn't gone long.

Silky strands of his hair brushed her cheek as he trailed hot kisses down her jaw. Her throat. He spent time sucking on the spot where her neck met her shoulder.

Chills erupted across her skin.

"Relax."

Then he pulled back the fleshy part of her mound, revealing her clitoris. Something small and firm rolled over her clit. Not Blake's tongue, as it was lapping her left nipple.

Willow's breath caught at the direct stimulation. Not cold, not hot, just constant.

After a few more circles around the throbbing flesh, the ball passed over her slit to stop at her opening. Blake's finger pushed the ball inside her channel, not deep, but far enough she knew it was there.

When she gasped, he murmured against her breast, "Bear down around my finger."

She squeezed.

"That's it. Damn you are so tight. And slick." His mouth meandered up to her ear and he blew gently. "I like that I can make you wet."

"Please. Blake—"

"Patience. It'll be worth it, I promise." He eased his finger out and began rubbing another one of those mysterious balls over her clit.

This time as he teased her with the ball, he suckled strongly on her nipples. Alternating sides with nips of his teeth and light, wet whips of his tongue.

He rolled it down her cleft, pausing at her entrance.

Willow held her breath as he inserted the second ball next to the first. She tightened her innermost muscles around his finger without him asking.

Blake groaned. "Jesus."

By the time the third ball began sliding across her clit, in that same maddening, arousing rhythm, she noticed something else. The aroma drifting up from her body. Her musk mixed with something syrupy sweet, like...cherries.

Her eyes flew open and she glanced down.

He smiled at her. "You obeyed longer than I thought you would."

"Are you...are those maraschino cherries?"

"Yep."

"But you're..."

"Playing with them. And playing with you. Let's call it the bartender's version of *Ben Wah* balls." He rolled the cherry through her wet folds and pushed it inside her. "Plus, cherries are my favorite fruit. Next to tastin' your sweet love fruit."

Willow's face heated. "Umm. How are you going to get them out?"

Blake fell to his knees. "With my tongue."

A little flutter started in her stomach and spread lower.

"Don't tense up. It won't hurt, I promise."

He clamped his fingers on her ass. He bent his head and placed his mouth over the mouth of her sex. He began to lick his way inside her pussy. His tongue stroked and he sucked, making soft happy noises.

That concentrated licking was beyond divine and she moaned her approval of his retrieval technique.

Just when Willow thought he'd never be able to reach far enough inside without burying his entire face in her, she felt the cherries slide down a fraction. "Oh."

Blake lifted his face and grinned. Between his teeth was one maraschino cherry. He closed his eyes and bit down on it, making a growling sound. "Juicy. One down, two to go."

She whimpered.

Cherry number two rolled right into his hungry mouth.

The third cherry proved difficult to extricate and Blake spent more time sucking than licking.

Not that Willow complained. In fact, she was a having a hard time getting her brain to focus on anything besides the words *wet, hot, more.*

Once the fruit was within reach, Blake curled that talented tongue around it and slurped it into his mouth. "Mmm."

Willow watched him chew and swallow, wondering what he was thinking. Would he give her a play-by-play of what he planned to do to her next? Or would he ask her what she wanted?

Neither.

Blake slid his hands up the inside of her thighs. He bent his head and fastened his mouth to her clit.

After all the teasing and build up, his relentless attention to that swollen bead set her off. She came fast. She came hard. Waves of pleasure crashed over her, until she slumped against the wall, her arms too wobbly to keep her upright.

Through her ragged breathing and pounding heart, she heard Blake stand. His hands, smelling of cherries and of her, curled around her face. She blinked up at him.

"I need to fuck you. Now." He lifted her off the stool as if she weighed nothing.

Willow wrapped her body around his, still half-shaky, still a little unsure on his plans.

He took her to the end of the bar where a brass handrail separated the waitress station from the counter. He buried his face in her neck. "I wanted to take my time with you, but I'm too far gone to be gentle or easy or slow."

"Whatever you want."

Blake spun her around and set her on her feet. "Grab onto the rails."

She heard the chink of his buckle loosening. The zip of his zipper lowering. The rustle of his pants sliding down. The crinkle of the condom wrapper as he put it on.

All sexy sounds that rebuilt her desire to fever pitch.

Then his mouth was by her ear and his hands were on her hips. "Bend over and grab onto the rails. Good. Now put your feet on the tops of my boots."

Blake had a wide stance. And when she stepped up, she knew why. His sex was perfectly aligned with hers. The tip of his cock circled her entrance once and plunged in. "Sweet Jesus do you feel like heaven, Will." He pulled out. "Hot." He slammed back in. "Tight." Back out. "Wet." Back in. "Perfect."

She held on, giving herself over to the moment, giving herself over to this man. Tingles radiated from a spot deep inside her, awakening the tight, achy knot of need, warning something explosive was about to be unleashed.

"Do you know how sexy you look? With your skirt flipped up? With the way you arch toward me every time I push into you?"

"Blake—"

"I can't hold back. I need..." His strokes quickened. Deepened. Then Blake shouted and his cock jerked inside her. He groaned when she squeezed his thick shaft with her interior muscles.

Enthralled with his primitive response, she didn't notice his hand dipping between her legs until he started lightly thrusting again in time to his stroking finger.

"Come for me." He canted his pelvis, changing the angle so the head of his cock rubbed inside on the spot below her pubic bone.

Willow lost it. Her pussy and clit pulsed together, sending her into an orgasm that robbed her of breath.

Through the sexual haze floating over her she felt Blake place his hands over hers on the rail. He murmured, "Now I know the real reason you were crowned Miss Firecracker. Damn woman, you are explosive."

"Seems a great big match is what it takes to set me off."

He laughed and brushed his lips across the back of her head. "Please come upstairs with me."

She liked that he didn't assume. "I'd like that."

Chapter Eight

Blake led Willow up the dark staircase to the apartment.

What about Willow brought out his beastly side? He'd never acted so aggressive. Was he giving her something to remember him by? Or a reason for her to ask him to stick around?

And Willow's uninhibited response had stunned him. Especially dropping to her knees and sucking him off in the storeroom with a bar full of people right outside the door.

She stopped abruptly, knocking him slightly off balance. He turned but he could hardly see her. "What's wrong?"

"You weren't even listening to me."

"Sorry. You're right."

"You aren't going to lie?"

"I don't lie. Besides, what'd be the point?" Blake backed down a couple of steps until they were almost eye-to-eye. "But I will give you an excuse."

"What?"

"I was thinking about you. How sexy it was you were all in for the games we played." He tucked a stray hair behind her ear. "I can't wait to do it again. Does that make me a pig?"

Willow watched him intently.

Blake kept stroking his thumb over her temple. "Will?"

"I've never met anyone like you," she blurted.

"Is that good or bad?"

"Good. I think. But being with you makes me want to do very bad things."

"Things are only bad if they're illegal or if someone gets hurt. And as far as I can tell, nothin' you and I have done qualifies on any level."

She retained a skeptical look and Blake figured he needed to lighten up.

He smooched her forehead, her nose, her chin and her throat. "You hungry?"

"You'd cook for me at two in the morning?"

"I'd cook for you anytime you asked, sunshine. So, how about a buffalo chicken wrap?"

"Sounds yummy. I am pretty starved," she admitted.

"I'll fix you up."

Inside the apartment, Blake flipped on the lamps in the living room. He glanced at her and grinned. "Let me slip into something more comfortable and clean up before I get busy cooking."

"Feeling a little sticky?"

Blake let his gaze drop between her thighs. "No more sticky than you are I imagine."

That got her. She blushed.

He smiled again. Smirked really. "Make yourself at home. I'll be right back."

Blake ended up jumping in the shower. After running a comb through his tangled curls, he slipped on a baggy pair of faded cargo shorts and a sleeveless T-shirt with "Healing Touch Massage" emblazoned on the front.

He saw her sifting through the pile of paperbacks on the coffee table. "Bathroom's all yours."

Without turning around, she asked, "Are these your books?"

"Yeah."

"Have you read all of them?"

"Most of 'em."

"Really?"

Why did she sound surprised he liked to read?

Willow held up a thriller. "What did you think of this one?"

He shrugged. "Left me a little cold. Seemed the author wanted me to know he'd done his research. Too much worthless information in it." He paused. "Have you read it?"

"I started it, but I put it down after I stumbled across the first sex scene." Her shoulders shook with a mock shudder. "It was horrible. Very unrealistic."

"No kidding."

She shoved it on the table and picked up the next book in the stack. "And this one?"

"Now that one... What's not to love about a kick-ass female character?"

"Wasn't it great?"

"Uh-huh. Now the sex scene, above the bar?" He whistled. "Totally smokin' hot."

"Yeah, I could totally see it happening," Willow added.

They realized simultaneously they were above a bar. A bar in which they'd just had smokin' hot sex. And if Blake had his way, they would have some more smokin' hot sex.

Willow set the book down and looked at him. "I get a lot of crap from the guys for reading."

"Me too."

They just stood there at smiled at each other.

"Well, I'd better get to it." Blake sidestepped her and headed into the small kitchen. He heard the bathroom door close.

He sliced the cooked chicken breasts and tossed them in a pan with tangy buffalo sauce. While that heated, he chopped lettuce. He spread blue cheese dressing on the wheat tortilla, added a line of chicken and sauce. The final step before he rolled them was sprinkling on lettuce and cheddar cheese.

"That smells yummy."

"I hope you like it. Would you like something to drink?"

"Water. I'll get it."

"No. Sit. It'll just take a sec."

Blake slid the plates on the table, poured them each a glass of water and grabbed the container of veggies out of the fridge.

Willow looked at him dumbfounded as he sat across from her.

He bristled. "What?"

"Fresh cut veggies? Carrots and celery. Cauliflower and broccoli. Radishes and...are those sugar snap peas?"

"Yeah. Why, do you hate 'em or something?"

She placed her hand on his forearm. "I love them. I just never...well, I never think of going to this kind of trouble. And I see that you do. This isn't just for my benefit, is it? You eat like this all the time?"

His cheeks warmed. "It doesn't take more time to have this kind of stuff on hand than a bag of chips. And I've gotten really conscious of what I eat since my dad's stroke." Dammit. He hadn't meant to tell her that.

"Oh Blake. I'm sorry. When did it happen?"

"It happened a few months back."

"Is he okay?"

"He's getting better but not good enough. We had to sell—" No. He would not tell her that. "Anyway, it changed a lot of things in my life. With the West family history of men having heart attacks, strokes and dying at an early age, I'm becoming more vigilant about all aspects of my health."

Her hand lightly, soothingly stroked his forearm. "I am sorry. I don't know what I'd do if something like that happened to my dad. I worry about him. But he's the type you can't tell anything."

"Sounds familiar. But now my dad *has* to listen." He pointed to her plate. "Better eat."

"Bossy." Willow took one bite and moaned.

His cock stirred with awareness at her sexy sound. Damn. She made that noise right before she came.

She chewed and swallowed. "That is absolutely delicious."

"Glad you think so." Blake watched as she ate every bite and a big helping of veggies.

"What a day." She drooped in her chair. "Amazing sex. Amazing food. You've spoiled me, Blake West."

"I aim to please, ma'am." He gathered the plates. As he rinsed the dishes, Willow scooted in behind him and pressed her face in the middle of his back. She didn't say a word; she just hugged him for a minute or two. Then she hip-checked him, snagged a dishtowel and started drying.

Right then Blake knew he was in big trouble with this pint-sized woman.

When they finished, Willow faced him with a jaw-cracking yawn. "Will you be disappointed if I just want to go to sleep?"

"Hmm. Lemme think." He kissed the top of her head. "Nope. I'm pretty whupped myself." He steered her toward the bedroom.

"I have to be at the jobsite at seven which is in another four hours. Do you have an alarm clock so I can get up on time?"

"I'll get you up, I promise."

"Won't you want to sleep in?"

She was probably thinking he led the leisurely life of a bartender. Work late; sleep late. He laughed. "I've never had the luxury."

"Sucks to be you." She stripped and crawled between the sheets. "Blake? You coming to bed?"

"Yeah."

"Fully clothed?"

"Might be safer. Your nekkid body next to my nekkid body is *not* a sign my body reads as naptime."

Willow threw back the covers. She stood and reached for a T-shirt hanging over the back of the chair. She slipped it over her head and it hung to her knees. "Happy?"

"No. I like you nekkid." Blake stripped off his shirt, loving the way her eyes ate him up. He took two condoms out of his front pocket and set them on the dresser. "In case you change your mind."

She snorted.

His cargo shorts hit the floor, leaving him in his boxer briefs.

He scrambled beside her and she curled around him, sighing sleepily against his chest. After a couple minutes, she murmured, "I like you nekkid too. But that's not the reason I like you, Blake."

"What is the reason, sunshine?"

"You make me feel like I'm the sexiest woman alive."

"You are."

Willow sighed again. "See? That sweet side of you isn't fake.

221

You're almost too good to be true. There has to be something you're not telling me."

Blake stroked her back and listened to her breathe. As she floated off he was glad he didn't have to answer.

As usual, he came out of a dead sleep at six a.m. Willow didn't stir even when he shifted his arm out from underneath her. For the next half hour, he laid there staring at the ceiling fan, trying to will his hard-on away.

Wake her up. She'll help you get rid of it.

No. Be a gentleman. Wake her up and get her out of here.

Sound, safe advice. But Blake liked how Willow curled into him. He really liked the sweet scent of her skin. And her soft breath flowing across his chest.

Yeah, thinking about how good she felt and smelled wasn't deflating his morning wood at all.

Blake counted to one hundred. Three times. Then he nudged her. "Will? It's time to get up."

No response.

"It's past time to hit the road."

A sleepy groan.

He put his mouth by her ear. "Come on, sleepyhead."

If anything, she snuggled closer.

So Blake touched her. Sliding his hands under her shirt and tracing the vertebra of her spine. Palming the taut globes of her ass, marveling at how soft her bare skin felt beneath his rough-skinned hands.

Willow began to stir.

He upped the ante, slipping his fingers around the side of her breast. He wondered if he suckled her sweet nipples if she'd wake up fast or slow.

Now was as good as time as any to try it out.

Blake rolled her flat, bunched the T-shirt in his fist and set his mouth on her. No delicate butterfly licks. He started out full bore, balls to the wall, with hard, deep sucking.

She gasped. "Blake? What are you—"

He slurped her nipple. Then scraped his teeth across the tip. "I'm waking you up."

"But—"

"I figured you'd prefer this to me throwing cold water on you."

"Mmm." Willow stretched. "Or you could wake me up like you did yesterday morning."

"That was next on the list if this didn't work." Blake flicked his tongue around the outer edge of her areola.

"This is a good alternative."

He lavished attention on her breasts until she writhed beneath him. He scattered kisses up her chest and muttered, "I want you," against her throat.

"Yes. Now."

Blake was suited up in no time. He kept kissing her neck as he moved between her thighs. Willow wrapped her legs around his hips and arched into him as he slipped into her damp heat.

Her fingers mapped the muscles in his arms and back in a languorous caress that appeased and inflamed him.

Their movements against each other were unhurried. A lazy melding of bodies as the morning sun lightened the room and the ceiling fan stirred the sex-scented air around them.

This was the perfect way to wake up. Blake could get very used to a soft, willing Willow in his bed every morning.

Her breathy moan in his ear and the vise-like grip of her

pussy muscles as she climaxed around his thrusting cock sent him soaring.

When he landed, he brushed his lips over her temple. "Can you stay for breakfast?"

"What time is it?"

"After seven."

"What!" Willow tried to push him away. "Why didn't you wake me?"

"I tried. It didn't work, which was why I had to come up with a more...innovative method." Blake lifted slightly to look at her. "Besides, you're already late so you might as well stick around and eat."

"But—"

"How many times have you been late to the jobsite, boss lady?"

"Hardly ever."

"So you're entitled." He pressed his lips to hers. "Please. Stay. Just a little bit longer. I'm thinking of three little words that'll make it worth your while."

Her eyes lit with wariness and Blake could've kicked himself for scaring her.

Keep it light. He said, "Ham." Another soft peck. "Pancakes." Another kiss. "Eggs."

She relaxed. "You trying to fatten me up?"

"Nope. But I'll sweeten the pot. I'll even throw in fresh coffee and a side of sliced strawberries."

"You drive a hard bargain, Blake." Willow smiled. "Lemme up so I can call my crew."

By the time Willow appeared in the kitchen, breakfast was nearly done.

"I still have to stop at home and load up my tools." She

stuffed a big bite of pancakes into her mouth and made that little happy moan. Yep. His dick stirred.

Blake gave her a once over. "It might be hard to nail siding in that skirt, but damn, is it perfect for me nailing you." Her answering blush was cute as hell.

"So what are your plans today?" she asked.

He speared a hunk of ham. "I guess Mondays are slow, so I'll probably work in the office, do inventory, at least until the happy hour crowd shows up."

"I oughta work in the office today too," she admitted, "but I'll probably do it later tonight."

"You could bring your office work over here and we could do the drone work together."

Willow rolled her eyes. "We'd never get a lick of work done."

"And that's what makes the idea all the more appealing."

"You are a bad influence on me. Bribing me with food. What's next? Sex?"

"Uh-huh. I'm thinking about bending you over the table and having my wicked way with you before you race off."

Her fork froze midair. "Blake West."

He grinned when he realized she hadn't said no. "Besides, you're already late, what's another half hour?"

Willow slowly set her fork down. She shoved her plate to the middle of the table. Wiped her mouth with a napkin and pushed to her feet. She started down the hallway.

"Hey, Will? Where you goin'?"

She whirled around. "To get a condom. You'd better hurry and finish eating so you can clear the table before I get back."

Blake lost his appetite, his train of thought and any chance he'd finish with her in thirty lousy minutes.

❖

Willow was dead on her feet. She hadn't worked a full nine-hour shift, but she had tried to make up for lost time once she'd hit the jobsite.

Three hours late.

Lord. Blake's half an hour of playtime had stretched into two hours. By the time he'd coated her body with syrup, licked it all off and taken his own sweet, sticky time making love to her, they'd both needed a shower.

Once Willow was faced with soaping Blake's big, hard body and bulging muscles, well, racing off to work had been the dead last thing on her mind. She'd worked over one big, hard muscle in particular until he'd whimpered.

Yes, that shower had been refreshing in oh-so-many ways.

Still...she was tired. No sleep, indulging in more sex in the last two days than she'd had in her entire twenty-five years tuckered a girl out. She had every intention of driving straight home and snuggling between her sheets.

So why did she find herself cruising down Main Street?

Because the man was like a damn drug.

She inched past LeRoy's Tavern. Holy moly. The place was hopping for a Monday night. Mandy was probably raking in killer tips.

I don't work on Mondays.

If Mandy wasn't around that meant Blake was doing everything by himself.

Willow hit the brakes, spun a u-turn and bumped into the rear parking lot. The back door was unlocked. Her clothes were filthy. She pulled one of Mandy's extra blouses from her locker and slipped on the denim skirt she'd had in her duffel bag, ignoring the teasing scent of cherries. After she scrubbed her hands, she headed up front.

Blake was inundated.

Even Boy Scouts needed a little help now and then.

He didn't acknowledge her until she'd sidled up beside him. "What do you want me to do?"

"Will? What're you...?" Blake ran the back of his hand across his face. "If you'd handle the bottled beer that'd be great. Happy hour prices are two bucks domestic, three bucks import."

"Got it." Willow let out a wolf whistle. The noise in the bar dropped a level. "If you're looking for bottled beer, the line forms here."

"What about well drinks?" a man demanded.

She pointed to Blake. "He'll get your order. And if you want something frou-frou, like a blended daiquiri or a piña colada, you're in the wrong bar."

Laughter rang out.

For the next hour, Willow uncapped beer bottles, hauled ice and restocked. Blake was still a bit frazzled, but he never snapped at her or at a customer. His smile wasn't as wide as she'd seen it other nights, but the man was still smiling.

Especially when he glanced her way. A very satisfied male expression transformed his face. But oddly enough, it wasn't sexual in origin.

Once they'd caught up, she propped her elbows on the bartop. "I guess people pour in for the drink specials, huh?"

"Appears that way." Blake drained a bottle of water and stared at her.

"What?"

"I'm surprised to see you."

She shrugged.

"The last thing I heard after you totally fried my circuits in the shower this mornin' was that you wouldn't be around tonight."

"I hadn't planned on it until I drove by the bar and saw you were swamped. I remembered Mandy wasn't working. I figured you could use the help."

Blake didn't toss out a funny comment or offer her a dimpled grin; he just kept studying her with those intense hazel eyes.

"What?"

"Is that the only reason you came by?"

Willow never thought of herself as shy. But with the knowing way Blake considered her, she had the unusual urge to duck her face from his scrutiny.

"Will?"

"No, that's not the only reason."

He waited for her response. Just as she knew he would.

"I'm here because I missed you. I-I can't seem to stay away from you." She glanced down at her boots.

Blake put his fingers under her chin, lifting her face to meet his gaze. "Did you know how crazy I am about you?"

Willow shook her head.

"You do now." He kissed her square on the mouth.

The knots in her belly loosened.

"Stay with me tonight?" he whispered against her lips.

She nodded.

Last call couldn't come soon enough.

Blake closed the bar at ten o'clock. He disappeared in the

back while she tidied up the front. When Willow ventured to the office, all the lights were off. The heavy steel door slammed and the deadbolts clicked. Blake smiled and took her hand, leading her upstairs.

In the apartment he rubbed his hands up and down her arms. "You hungry?"

"Um. No. Thanks."

"Come on then." Clasping her hand, he guided her into the bedroom.

Willow stopped in the doorframe. Candles were scattered around the room, giving off a golden glow and a mix of scents. The bedding was stripped back to just white sheets. "What... Wow. When did you have time to do this?"

"You like it?"

"I love it. I've never..." *Had a man try to impress me with romance.* Especially not when she was a sure thing.

"I wondered if you'd find this clichéd."

She faced him. "No! But you didn't have to go to all this trouble."

"And yet I did." Blake tugged her against his body, pressing his hands in the small of her back. "It's been a few crazy days. I wanted to slow it down a bit tonight."

She blinked at him.

"What?"

"You're so thoughtful."

"I try."

"I don't deserve this."

He frowned. "Why not?"

"Because I can't reciprocate." She groaned with frustration. "I'm bad at gooey romantic stuff. I never know what I'm supposed to be doing."

"You knew exactly what you were doing earlier in the shower." He placed his lips on her temple and murmured, "Amazingly hot, Will."

"Blake—"

"Ssh. Let me see you." He undressed her. Kissing each section of newly bared skin.

"I'm glad you don't want a strip tease," she mumbled between his flirty kisses.

"I'll admit I woulda liked to've seen you whipping your undies up on the ceiling fan. I was surprised you put the sash back on once you were nekkid."

"Not exactly queenly behavior. Then again, I was hardly the epitome of beauty queen."

"You're the epitome of beauty to me. From what I've seen, you're definitely a firecracker. So the title fits you." Blake slid the straps of her bra down her biceps and she shivered at the raw sensuality in his eyes.

"I'm definitely explosive when you touch me."

"I've got a short fuse when it comes to you." He whispered, "On the bed."

Willow rested on her elbows and watched him strip. She whistled. "I'll bet you could make a mint in a strip club with that hot, sexy body of yours."

Blake slipped on a condom and hung on all fours above her. "I can't imagine having dozens of chicks grabbing my junk."

"All that attention isn't a little bit appealing?"

"Nope. I only want one woman's hands on me."

"Really? Do I know her?"

"Uh-huh."

"Is it...me?" she asked with mock shock.

"Yep. 'Cause, sunshine, you are an expert in handling certain...tools."

She giggled.

He kissed her. Drawing out every ounce of pleasure with just his mouth on hers. He feathered his lips across her jawbone. Her cheek. Her eyelids. Her eyebrows. Her forehead. He nuzzled her hairline.

Then Blake let his mouth, his hands, his breath, even the ends of his hair caress her skin. Purposely avoiding the area between her thighs. He traced her bikini line and the crease of her leg with the very tip of his tongue.

Her body shook. Her blood pumped hot and fast. She was actually dizzy. With want. With need. For him. For what he brought to her. For how he made her feel.

He whispered, "Let's sit up." He stretched his legs out in front of him, maneuvering her across his lap, her knees on either side of his hips.

Willow panicked. "Wait. Blake. I've never done it this way... I don't know what I'm doing."

"Do what you want. Do what feels good. I'm gonna be touching you everywhere while you figure it out."

She didn't waste time, she immediately impaled herself.

He groaned. She groaned. And so it began. The glide of skin on skin. Long kisses. Short kisses. Sighs. Tasting. Touching. The erotic dance started slow, developing heat and speed until their sweat-slicked bodies were slamming together.

Blake thrust up when Willow pressed down. His marauding mouth was on her neck, her breasts, her shoulders. It seemed to be everywhere at once.

Her body was primed to shatter. Each hip bump, each grinding downstroke, each sucking kiss, each bead of sweat created between them brought her closer to that elusive breaking point.

Blake said "Come on, Will. Come for me. Take me with you this time." His hand slipped between their bodies and he rapidly thumbed her clit.

She detonated. His mouth remained sucking on her throat, sending a connective wave from her pulsing sex to her throbbing nipples. "Blake? Oh God. Oh God!"

Her muscles tightened around his cock, but he didn't shift or change his strokes, he rode out the storm with her.

Then Blake had his hands on her ass. Frantic thrusts gave way to stillness. She watched as he threw his head back and came with a drawn out groan.

Slumped together, they held each other, trying to retain some semblance of sanity.

Finally, Willow lifted her face from the spot on his shoulder that seemed tailor-made for her head.

Their eyes met.

She whispered, "Kaboom."

He whispered back, "Definitely kaboom."

Chapter Nine

Willow thought about Blake all morning. How he'd done so many sweet, considerate things for her. She wanted to repay him and prove she wasn't inept when it came to romantic gestures.

The candles, the music, the seduction last night...pure romance. Pure Blake.

At the sandwich shop she bought two supreme meat and veggie subs, two cups of potato dumpling soup and two chocolate macadamia nut cookies. Not exactly healthy, but the man had to indulge once in a while.

She entered through the service door. "Blake?"

He poked his head out of the office. "Willow? What're you doin' here?"

She held up the box with the food. "Lunchtime."

"I was hoping you were here to offer me a nooner."

"It depends on how fast you eat."

"Don't tempt me, sunshine." He kissed the top of her head and took the box. "Let's eat in the bar. Hopefully the delivery I'm waiting on will show up while we're eating, so afterward I can sneak you upstairs for a quickie before you head back to the trenches."

Willow balanced on the tips of her steel-toed boots and

smooched his chin. "You have the best ideas."

Soon as she'd divided the food, Blake straddled her across his lap and kissed her thoroughly. "Mmm. That's what I was hungry for. It's been forever since I tasted your sweet kisses."

"Forever? It's been four hours since you kissed me goodbye."

"Like I said. Forever." Then Blake kissed her again.

Willow sighed. "You're heating me up while the food's getting cold."

"That's how it should be." But he set her on her own chair.

Blake wiped his mouth and spun to face her. "What are you doin' tonight?"

"I don't know. Why?"

"I know you have to work early tomorrow, and it'd be late, but could I come by your place tonight after the bar closes?"

"Sure. What's going on?"

Blake smoothed back the hair that'd fallen from her ponytail. "We need to talk about some stuff."

"Like what?"

"Like...what happens when Dave comes back."

Her stomach did a little flip.

"And some other stuff that I don't want to talk about here, okay?"

"Okay."

He tucked into his sandwich. She stared into her soup, her appetite completely gone.

Willow thought she'd be prepared for the "it's been fun" speech, but she now realized she didn't want him to go.

Maybe he doesn't have to.

Before she lost her nerve, she blurted, "If you need a job

when you're done working for Dave, you can come to work for me."

His mouth dropped open.

"You've done construction and we're always looking for reliable workers, especially carpenters, and you might not be working with me, but I'm sure we could find some way to put your skills to use."

"Willow. That's not—"

She put her fingers over his lips. "Just think about it, okay?"

The back door slammed. But it wasn't a delivery person pushing a handcart full of beer through the doorway. It was Dave LeRoy. Holding a duffel bag and looking annoyed.

"Dave? What the hell? You were supposed to be gone another couple days."

"Nice to see you too."

"Something go wrong?"

"Might say that. The fishing sucked. Gloria was being a first-class b—" he glanced at Willow and amended, "—baby, and I decided enough was enough."

"What happened?"

"We broke up."

"Aw man, that sucks."

"Tell me about it. So I tucked my tail between my legs and slunk home like the whipped dog I am. You're off the hook."

Would Blake just up and leave now that Dave was back?

Dave dropped the duffel bag. "The hook comment would've been funnier if my fishing trip hadn't gone in the crapper."

"Isn't a crapper a fish?" Blake asked.

"That'd be a crappie. Which also describes my mood."

"Why don't you head on upstairs? I've got it covered down here."

"Nah. I'm wired." Dave wandered behind the bar, helping himself to a glass of Sprite. He frowned at Willow. "I didn't think this was your kind of place."

She froze. Would Blake tell Dave what'd happened in his bar in his absence?

Then Dave looked back and forth between Blake and Willow. "You two know each other?"

"Startin' to. Maybe you oughta—"

"I get it." A huge smile bloomed on Dave's face. "You're cozying up to the competition, West. Smart."

"Competition?" Willow repeated.

Blake went board stiff next to her.

"Sure. Blake's a helluva carpenter. His skills have been wasted working part-time for his cousins. Now that his years as a sheep rancher are over, I'm trying to talk him into remodeling this place. Putting in a kitchen so I can serve bar food. Then he could hang out his shingle, so to speak."

"Dave—"

"You're a sheep rancher?" Willow said incredulously.

Dave laughed. "Now why am I not surprised you kept that to yourself?" He confided in Willow, "Bet he didn't tell you he and his dad just sold their spread for a pile of money?"

"No. He neglected to mention that." She spun toward Blake. "So you're not 'between jobs'? You're not really a bartender?"

"I am a bartender, Will," Blake said softly. He looked at her. "Does it matter?"

"It does if you're a carpenter with unlimited funds, pretending to be a bartender, so you can get the lowdown on what it'd take to compete with us."

"A little competition would do Gregory Construction some good," Dave said.

"Shut up," Willow and Blake snapped simultaneously.

"I'm just sayin'..." Dave put up his hands. "It's obvious you two have some things to talk about." He disappeared into the back.

Things started to click into place. Blake asking her specific details about their business. Their main focus. How many guys worked for them. She was amazed *he* hadn't suggested she patch the wall, not to lessen the amount she owed for bar damage, but so he could ascertain her skill level.

Infuriated, she jumped to her feet. "You totally played me."

"How do you figure?"

"Getting me to talk about my job."

"And that means I have ulterior motives? Because I'm interested in your life?"

"Darn right it does. When you haven't been honest with me about yours." Her cheeks burned with embarrassment. "Are you having a good laugh about me asking you to come to work for us? Cozying up to the owner? Was that your plan from the start?"

Blake smacked his hands on the counter. "When you barged in here I had no idea who you were besides a confrontational drunk who also happened to be Miss Firecracker. The local beauty queen, not the local carpenter."

"You slept with me under false pretenses!"

"What was false about it? That I think you're sexy, smart, funny and sweet? That you look as hot in a toolbelt as you do in a pageant sash? That I like spendin' time with you in and out of bed?" His eyes glittered. "Lemme tell you something, sunshine, there was nothin' false about my cock getting hard every time I saw you or touched you."

"That is not the point."

"What is the point?"

"You lied about being between jobs."

"I *am* between jobs."

"You didn't tell me you had money."

"Maybe it's because I'm not used to having money. Or maybe I kept it quiet because I'd like a woman to be attracted to me—not to my bank account."

"You know I'm not like that!"

"And you know I am not a liar." Blake sighed. "Look, I've gotten used to women pretending to like me for other reasons. Hoping I'll introduce them to my good lookin' wild McKay cousins. Or because they expect I'll sneak them free drinks. Or sweet-talk me into doin' their home repairs for nothin'.

"The reason I didn't tell you about the years I spent a sheep rancher? That's not who I am, anymore than Miss Firecracker is who you are. It's afforded me some opportunities. Just like the title did for you. So I didn't lie. I *was* a carpenter. I *was* a sheepherder. But right now? I am *just* a bartender."

Her stomach clenched at his defeated tone.

Blake slid from the stool. "I didn't play you. I don't have plans to ruin your business by being in your bed. I am a decent guy who is tired of defending my livelihood at every turn to people who don't judge me as hard as I judge myself, no matter if I'm herding sheep, or nailing trim, or making drinks. I'm tired of explaining myself. I thought I didn't have to with you. I thought you were the first woman who saw me—the real me— who looked beyond labels, because you defy every one that's ever been put on you."

He wouldn't even look at her.

"Was I wrong, Willow?"

Dave poked his head around the corner. "Blake. Phone."

Blake sighed and started to walk away.

Don't go.

Willow stared after him. Confused. Heartsick. And feeling the unwelcome urge to cry.

Talk to him.

Forget him. He's leaving anyway.

She exited through the front door at a dead run and didn't look back.

Blake raced out the service entrance only to see gravel flying as Willow roared off in her truck.

"Fuck!"

He flipped open his cell phone to call her, to demand she get her ass back here so they could talk this out, when he realized he didn't have her cell phone number.

"Fuck."

"Standing in the parking lot and swearing at the memory of her tailgate ain't gonna do you any good, West."

Blake slumped against the building. "Think I don't know that, Dave?" He glanced over at his friend. "Perfect timing, by the way."

Dave laughed. "I sincerely hope you aren't blaming your stupidity on me."

"It might've been easier if I'd had the chance...shit. I had lots of chances. I didn't take any of 'em. I totally fucked this up."

"Yep."

"Thanks for the support."

"Anytime. So you and Willow Gregory, huh?"

"I don't wanna talk about her."

Dave handed him a bottle of water. "Okay. Then can I ask you something else?"

No.

"Why the big secret about being a sheep rancher? Why've you always been embarrassed about it?"

"Maybe it's all the jokes. 'Wyoming. Where men are men and sheep are nervous.' Or maybe it's because the rest of my family, on both the West and McKay side, are cattle ranchers. Successful ranchers and we've always struggled. Or maybe it's because my brother bailed on the ranch as soon as he could and left me with no choice but to stay on and help Dad."

"You could've left."

Blake shook his head. "We barely scraped by most years, so no way could he afford to hire help if I left. What was I supposed to do? Act like the sheep business he'd devoted his life to wasn't good enough for me? Act ungrateful?"

But weren't you doing that by hiding how you've spent the majority of your life?

"No. But instead you made yourself miserable?"

"I didn't hate working on the ranch. Not like Nick. It was just what I did, kinda like washing bar glasses. It's not exciting, but you just do it anyway without thinking about it because it needs done."

"Okay. I get that. So was it the same 'I don't wanna be ungrateful' story when you learned carpentry?"

"Sort of." He cracked the lid on the water bottle and took a long drink. "Except I'd bet a hundred bucks that my cousins Chet and Remy only offered to teach me because they felt sorry for me."

"Why?"

"After Nick left, they thought I'd gotten trapped in a life I hadn't chosen."

"Weren't you?"

"I hadn't thought of it that way until I started working for them. So yeah, the upside was I learned a new skill set, but I got the impression they felt they were doing me a favor, ya know?"

"I hear ya. But again, you were too nice a guy to say no when they asked you for help?"

"Pretty much."

Dave sighed. "You ever done anything *you've* wanted to do job-wise? Without worrying about whether your decision will hurt a family member's feelings? Or without being embarrassed about what you're doing?"

"The only job I've ever gotten on my own was at the Rusty Spur. I like tending bar. I'm good at it."

"I wouldn't have asked you to watch my place if I didn't know that."

"Thanks."

A bout of silence stretched between them.

"Look, I wasn't blowing smoke the night I talked about expanding LeRoy's. With the storefront next door empty, I could add on a kitchen. Probably start out serving bar food and see how that goes."

"I imagine it'll go over well."

Dave tossed his empty water bottle in the recycling bin and jammed his hands in his pockets. "I know you're struggling to find a place to land after your dad's stroke. So I just wanna throw it out there that if you're interested, sincerely interested, not just being 'Blake the nice guy' to your old buddy Dave, but looking to make a permanent change in your life, well, I'd like to talk seriously about a partnership."

That surprised Blake. "Why?"

"I had nothing but time to think on the way back from Jackson Hole. I realized that Gloria was right about a lot of things."

"Like?"

"Like I don't have a life outside of the bar. Makes it worse since I live upstairs and I can't seem to get away from it. I need to. Soon." He squinted at the horizon. "We both work too damn hard, Blake. Be nice to share the workload."

"That is true."

Dave turned and grinned. "And the profits."

"Yeah, you do have the beginnings of a goldmine here." Blake pushed up from the wall. "I appreciate the offer. Can I crash at your place and keep pouring drafts for the next couple days while I'm considering it?"

"Absolutely." He hesitated. "Now can I say something about Willow?"

"Have at it."

"She's a door slammer. She gets pissed, she slams the door and she stomps away. Once she cools off, she'll come back around."

"And if she doesn't?"

"You've got an entire bar to drown your sorrows in." Dave slapped him on the back. "Come on. You're off the clock. Lemme buy you a drink."

"Deal."

Willow drove aimlessly. She passed by Mandy's house, but something—probably pride—stopped her from pulling in and pouring her heart out.

At that moment, Willow realized she'd been so focused on her job that she hadn't maintained many female friendships. Her best buddy, Cerise, had married a soldier and they were stationed in Germany. Sure, they kept in touch via email, but it wasn't the same as meeting in person and gorging on ice cream or margaritas.

The guys Willow worked with were...well, guys. Good guys, but none of them would appreciate her spilling her guts. Not even over a beer. Not even if she was buying the beer.

Willow could call her mother. She'd be secretly thrilled to hear her daughter finally had man troubles. Despite their polar opposite personalities, Willow got along great with her, which meant Mom would know immediately something was wrong. Which meant her dad would know. Which meant Dad would threaten to take action. Which was never a good thing.

You had a good thing with Blake.

Up until I found out he lied.

He didn't lie. He just didn't tell you everything.

He should have.

Since when do you have to know every little thing about someone within four days?

That thought jarred her. She'd never expected that before.

Besides, hadn't Blake said he needed to talk to you?

Crap. She'd forgotten that too.

What if he'd meant to tell you about his past?

Fine. But why was he embarrassed about raising sheep?

Why were you embarrassed about being Miss Firecracker?

Touché.

Especially since you told Blake right after you met that part of your life was over and didn't matter.

Hadn't Blake just said the same thing?

243

That's not who I am, anymore than Miss Firecracker is who you are.

Her heart nearly stopped. What if she'd made a big deal...out of nothing? What if she was looking for an excuse to break it off with him first because she knew Blake was leaving? What if she broke it off in a manner that hurt him? So there was no chance she'd be hurt in return? And if she ended it when she was ticked off about something he'd done, it'd be easier to handle anger than sorrow.

Wouldn't it?

No.

On no. Oh no no no. Had she just made a big mistake?

Blake was a good man. Truthfully, he was the nicest, most decent, honest, hardworking, thoughtful, sweet, caring, loving man she'd ever met.

Didn't you secretly believe the man was too good to be true?

Yes.

You don't deserve him.

Which didn't matter now because she probably lost him.

That's when the tears came. A flood so intense she had to pull over on the side of the road.

About five minutes into her crying jag, her cell phone pealed, "Who's Your Daddy?" Willow debated on answering it, but her father would keep calling until she picked up. He was perverse that way. She wiped her eyes on her sleeve and hit talk. "Hey, Dad."

"Hey, baby girl."

"When did you and Mom get back?"

"About an hour ago."

"How's Jackie?"

"*Jackson* is fine. He missed you. He says hey."

"I miss him too. I wish I could've gone to meet his new football coach, but someone had to hold down the fort, right?"

"Speaking of...I stopped over at the Stone jobsite. The guys said you've been gone since before noon. You run into problems?"

"No."

"Huh. You sound funny. Is everything all right?"

No. Willow directed her anger and frustration at her father. "Maybe I sound funny because my dad is checking up on me first thing. Did you think I was slacking while you're gone?"

"Hell no. I just talked to the guys—"

"I work hard in this company, day in, day out, and if I want to take a long lunch or time to clear my head, I don't appreciate the guys tattling on me to you like I'm some juvenile delinquent—"

"Whoa, whoa, whoa, wait just a damn minute, Willow. I trust you and you damn well know it. The guys mentioned it 'cause they're worried about you. They said you showed up late yesterday morning too. You never do shit like this."

"Sorry."

"I don't want an apology. I want you to tell me what's really goin' on."

She sniffed. "It's nothing. Forget it."

Pause. Then, "Does this have something to do with that bartender working at LeRoy's that Paul told me about?"

Stupid big mouth Paul. "Dad—"

"Is he there with you now?"

"No."

"Who is this guy? Paul said he saw you together at your house all lovey-dovey and you were doin' repairs in the bar."

"So?"

245

"So, is this guy using you?"

I don't know. Maybe I was using him.

"Since when do repairs include a stint working as a cocktail waitress?" he demanded.

"It's a long story. Besides, it's over." Her voice caught on the word *over.*

His angry pause burned her ear. "Sweet baby Jesus, Willow Rose Gregory. Are you...*cryin'*?"

She nodded her head yes but whispered, "No."

"What did that dumb fucker do to make you cry?"

Silence.

"Answer me."

"Drop it, Dad."

"The fuck I will. Goddammit where are you?"

"Let me talk to Mom."

"Like hell. You'll tell her to tell me to calm down and I don't wanna calm down. He makes you cry, I make him cry."

For crap's sake. She was twenty-five years old! "Don't you dare, Dad. I mean it—"

A scuffle erupted and Willow guessed her mother grabbed the phone. Then the dial tone rang in her ear.

Good. Her dad was protective and hotheaded, but her mother was the voice of reason. She'd keep him from acting rashly.

Too bad her mom hadn't been around earlier to keep her from doing the same.

Two hours later, Blake was working on a fairly decent drunk when the door slammed open like an angry bull had kicked it in. The cowbell crashed to the floor with a final dull clank.

The bar went utterly still.

He knew without turning who'd come for a piece of him.

Big Kenny Gregory.

Fucking awesome.

Blake tossed back the shot of tequila. He straightened his carriage to his full height of six foot three. He briefly wondered how bad Willow's dad could be. Or how big he could be. Given Willow's petite frame chances were good this guy bullied people with his mouth, not his size. He slowly spun his barstool around.

Holy freakin' shit.

The guy was at least six foot eight. He weighed a good three hundred and fifty pounds. He had shaggy, curly dark hair laced with streaks of gray and a matching ZZ Top beard, which made him look like an outlaw biker. Or a prison escapee. Or both.

He stalked toward Blake, wraparound shades obscuring his eyes. His black sleeveless T-shirt read "What the Fuck You Lookin' At?" Ropes of thick chains swooped from the front of his jeans to the wallet jammed in his back pocket. Chains which rattled against the gigantic knife clipped to the left side of his studded belt.

Before the heavy boot steps stopped, Blake stood. He wasn't meeting this guy halfway, but he sure as hell wasn't sitting on his ass.

Big Kenny ripped off his shades and loomed over Blake. "You the piece of shit who made my baby girl cry?"

"Yep."

Not the answer Big Kenny expected. "Least you ain't denying it. You'd better start talking, boy, about what you done, or I start breaking bones until you do."

"With all due respect, Big Kenny, what happened between Willow and me isn't your business, so back off."

"Who the fuck you think you're talking to, boy?"

"I ain't a 'boy' and Willow isn't a little girl. She's a woman who doesn't need her daddy to run interference in her personal life."

Big Kenny growled.

"But I see where she gets her temper. You get pissed off first, stomp away second and worry about the rest of it later. Am I right?"

No answer.

"In fact, I'll bet you a thousand bucks she didn't tell you what happened between us. Know why? Because that'd mean she'd actually have to...I dunno...*talk* about it. But fuck, that'd be too goddamn easy, wouldn't it? No, it's much more productive to make assumptions! Which was what I was tryin' to avoid from the get-go, but she's pretty damn quick to jump to conclusions and not so quick to listen to explanations." Blake's eyes narrowed. "Does she get that trait from you too?"

Big Kenny glared at him.

Blake couldn't seem to shut his mouth. He was tired of being the nice guy. Tired of being called a Boy Scout. Tired of being the understanding type. Tired of being the calm one. Tired of being the one who walked away rather than stay to fight.

Fuck that.

"I ain't gonna lie. I wanna throttle her."

"You've got a death wish by telling me that. If you touch one hair on her head—"

"For Christsake, chill out. I'd never hurt her. Do you have any idea how much it twisted my guts into knots to see pain in her eyes? Dammit, that tough little woman looked at me like I'd broken her favorite hammer."

"Did you?"

"No! It's just a stupid misunderstanding that would've taken like ten minutes to clear up, but she couldn't be bothered to stick around and hash it out. She had to leave!" Blake grabbed onto the front of Big Kenny's shirt. "Where the fuck did she go, huh?"

"Hands off. Now."

"Blake. Buddy. Take it easy. Sit down," Dave said from behind the bar.

"Shut the fuck up, Dave. I don't wanna sit down. I've been taking it easy for too goddamn long. I wanna clear at least one thing up in my life right now."

Blake locked his gaze to Big Kenny's. "Go ahead and beat the shit out of me. 'Cause I sure as fuck couldn't feel any worse. And if I've got goddamn bruises and scabs, maybe I won't feel like such a fucking pussy for letting that little slip of a thing knock me to my knees."

"Remember you asked for it," Big Kenny snarled.

Blake would've laughed if he hadn't felt like crying. Or if he hadn't been bracing himself for the impending ass kicking from Willow's larger-than-life father. "Bring it on."

But the big man just sighed. He clapped Blake on the shoulder so hard Blake winced. "Boy—I mean, Blake, is it?" Blake nodded. "Sit yo' ass down." He signaled to Dave. "Give us a bottle of Jack, two shot glasses and then scram."

Dave complied and then they were alone.

Big Kenny poured them each a shot. They didn't toast. But Blake knew drinking protocol: Keep up with Big Kenny, shot for shot, no matter what. He apologized to his stomach lining and knocked the first one back.

"Since Will ain't gonna tell me nothin', I'm asking you to explain everything." Big Kenny looked over his shot glass. "Everything G-rated that ain't gonna make me kill you on the spot."

So Blake started talking. He kept talking until he had to reach behind the bar for a glass of water. When he finished, he realized Big Kenny's expression hadn't changed the entire time. Crap. He finished his shot and cringed when Big Kenny poured him another.

"Lemme see if I've got this straight. She was so damn glad to get rid of that title she got shitfaced right afterward. She got belligerent. You kept her out of jail and she spent the night with you—"

"Nothing happened." That night, but he doubted Big Kenny would appreciate the clarification.

"And while you'd basically protected her from herself and from the other perverted men looking for a drunken piece of ass, she was working off her damages and the two of you became...friends."

"Yeah."

"She thought you were just a bartender."

"I am a bartender," he pointed out.

"At one point you told her you'd been employed in the construction business."

"Also the truth," Blake said. Hell, was Big Kenny going to go over every tiny detail of their conversation? Probably. Probably it wouldn't be wise to suggest they move on to coming up with a solution to the situation with Willow rather than rehashing the problem.

"So she thought you were an unemployed carpenter who was stuck slinging drinks."

"Yep."

"But at no time during the four days you spent with her did you tell her that you were a sheep rancher?"

"Nope."

"Why the fuck not?"

Blake swallowed another shot. "Do you know how many Wyoming sheep fucker jokes I've heard in my lifetime? Christ. For the first time ever I didn't have to explain what I used to do for a living isn't who I am." He looked over at Big Kenny. "I didn't lie: I just didn't think it mattered. I especially didn't say anything after Willow told me her theory on people who raise barnyard animals."

Big Kenny nodded. "Saved me a bundle she wasn't a horse fanatic like some of her friends when she was growing up."

"I imagine."

"So when Will found out about your shepherding past, including the fact you don't hafta work because you're loaded—"

"Loaded is stretching it," Blake replied dryly.

"Boy, I got a pretty fair idea what Wyoming ranch land is worth. Loaded ain't far off, is it?"

"I'll get by."

"Still, she got pissed off?"

Blake nodded.

"Man. That don't make no sense."

"Willow thought I'd played her. She tossed out this wild theory I was pretending to be down on my luck, hoping to earn her sympathy so she'd hire me. Then I could learn everything about your construction business to better compete with Gregory Construction."

Big Kenny gave Blake a menacing look. "Is that true?"

"Far from it. I don't know what the hell I'm doing with my

life on a day to day basis, let alone long term."

"Why's that?"

Blake briefly closed his eyes. "I've been pretty fucked up since my dad's stroke."

"Shit. That sucks."

"Yeah. I miss working with him, but I don't miss the work, which makes me feel guilty because ranching was his life. He wanted it to be mine. And being a rancher is all I've ever really known. For the first time in my life I have the money, the time and the freedom to do whatever I want and I can't decide what to do with any of it.

"So I came here, hoping to straighten some shit out. And I met her." Blake swallowed a shot. "Of all the gin joints in the world, she had to walk into mine."

No surprise Big Kenny's face held a blank stare.

"I'm crazy about her. I've never met anyone like her. I like that she makes me laugh almost as much as I love to hear her laughing. Sounds insane. I've known her a total of four days."

"I proposed to her mama four hours after we met."

"No shit?" Blake said, hating his words were starting to slur.

"No shit. I saw her in that hot little cheerleading outfit and I was done for. We had big plans. Move to one of the coasts. Live the lifestyle of the rich and famous. See the world. We couldn't wait to get out of Nebraska. 'Course, my senior year in college I wrenched my knee and couldn't go pro."

"Go pro?"

"Pro football after college. I played linebacker for the Cornhuskers."

That explained a lot.

"We moved back here. I didn't want to at first but it wasn't like either of us had any other place to go. I took over my dad's construction company, figuring I'd stick it out a decade or so and we'd move on to bigger and better things. Then Barbie and me started havin' kids."

Barbie. That explained a lot about Willow's mom too.

"We've been here thirty years."

"Regrets?"

"Nah. A man can't live in the past."

"So you understand why I wanted to put my past behind me and live in the now?"

"I believe I do."

"Think you can help me convince your daughter—"

Big Kenny raised his ham-sized hand, cutting him off. "Huh-uh. You're on your own with her."

"Great."

More shots were poured and consumed.

Finally Big Kenny spoke. "Much like your dad, I thought I'd pass the business on to my son." He scowled. "That boy...well, he never showed the interest in the construction biz that Will did. I never pushed my son to join the business or made him feel he didn't have a choice about what to do with his life. But Will? She wanted it. I'm damn proud of her. It ain't an easy road she's taken. I just want her to be happy." Big Kenny turned on his barstool.

Here it comes, Blake thought blearily.

"So the question is, do you got what it takes to make my Will happy?"

"Yessir."

"Prove it."

"How?"

Big Kenny propped his elbow up on the bar and gave Blake a nasty smile. "Let's arm wrestle."

Blake muttered, "I am so fucked."

Chapter Ten

Blake West woke up and realized covering his head with a lacy pillow did not muffle the pounding inside his skull.

He shifted slightly on the damp sheets. The pillow tumbled away. A shaft of sunlight nearly fried his retinas. He squeezed his eyelids shut and muttered, "I'm in hell."

"A hell of your own making you stupid jerk," an angry female said, way too close to his ear.

Willow.

Wait. Willow was...here?

Wait. Where *was* here?

Blake jackknifed, twisting toward the voice he thought he'd never hear again, especially in bed.

Ooh big mistake. Sharp pulses lanced his brain like pointy metal spikes. "Fuck. Fuck. Fuck."

"Serves you right. What were you thinking getting popped with my dad?"

"I'm thinking I was a lot nicer to you when *you* woke up with a hangover."

"Now see, there's another obvious difference between us."

Despite the ache behind his eyeballs, he peeled his eyes open, one squinty lid at a time. Such a sight for his poor sore eyes. Beautiful Willow. Less than two feet away. Scowling at him.

He grinned. He couldn't help it. He'd take her scowling. He'd take her any way he could get her.

"My Gawd. Even hungover you're leering at me."

"Darlin', I always leer at you."

She snorted. "What goes around comes around I guess. Except you're not wearing a sash, *darlin'*."

Blake looked down. Yep. He was buck-ass nekkid. Then he noticed the floral sheets. And the sweet lime scent surrounding him. He realized he was in her bedroom.

Time warp. How had he gotten here? The last thing he remembered, besides the confrontation with Willow, was sitting at the bar drinking and then...

His lungs seized up. Sweet Jesus. Willow's father had shown up mad as a nest of hornets. They'd talked. They'd yelled. They'd done a billion shots. And then he'd admitted how he felt about Big Kenny Gregory's baby girl. Probably in graphic detail. Damn. He was lucky he wasn't in traction. With blackened eyes. And broken teeth. He had the oddest urge to pat his groin to determine if he'd been castrated.

"Sucks, doesn't it?"

"What?"

"Having a complete mental blank about your previous night's activities."

Blake drawled, "Okay, Miss—"

"Don't say it. Don't even think it," she warned.

"Fine, Miss-I-got-cherry-bombed-one-freakin'-time, cut to the chase. How did I end up naked in your bed?"

"You really don't remember?" she said with a silken purr. "All you did? All you said?"

"No. But if you weren't bein' such a beautiful distraction

I—"

Willow briefly placed her finger over his mouth. "Ah. Ah. Ah. Don't go there, cowboy. That sweet talkin' mouth of yours ain't gonna get you outta trouble this time."

"Did my sweet talkin' ways convince you to kiss and make up with me last night?"

"Nope. But it was hard for me to say no after you stripped to nothing but those sexy dimples."

"Ah, hell, Willow, I hope I didn't—"

"Let me finish." Willow angled over him. "I prefer the man who demands I mount up and ride him like a stallion to be sober, not babbling about liking me more than his dog, or swearing he'd keep me happy between the sheets forever, or confessing he doesn't care that I'm a better carpenter than he is."

Aghast, he groaned, "*I* said all that?"

"Yep. After my mom and dad left."

"Your dad was here?"

"Who do you think carried you up to my bedroom?"

"Big Kenny did? I thought he hated my guts." Blake's voice dropped to a whisper. "I'm pretty sure he tried to kill me with Jack Daniels last night."

"Nah. He doesn't get drunk as a skunk with guys he hates. He just pounds the snot out of them."

"That's comforting."

"You were both pretty far gone by the time he called my mom to come pick you both up at LeRoy's."

"Why both of us?"

"Evidently he thought you and I needed to talk, so he brought you here."

"Did we talk?"

"No. Buddy, you passed out." She locked her gaze to his. "So tell me... Did you really arm wrestle my dad?"

A fuzzy memory teased the edges of his mind. "Maybe. Probably."

"He said you arm wrestled for...me. Like I was a prize at the fair or something."

Her hurt tone meant he had to do some major damage control. "Aw, you are the fairest prize I could ever hope to win, Willow Gregory."

"Sweet talker, but keep going."

"I remember trying to explain to your father why I wanted to throttle you and kiss you. Often at the same time. I guess he understood." Blake frowned. "After that, it's a blur."

"According to Dad, you beat him at arm wrestling."

"Huh. I wish I remembered."

"FYI, he never forgets. And he never loses."

"He had nothin' on me last night because I had nothin' to lose and everything to gain by winning." Blake caught her gaze. "I'm sorry."

"I know."

"I didn't mean to hurt you."

"I know."

"I wasn't playing you. I'm not that kind of guy."

She blinked at him.

"Please. Hear me out. I wasn't trying to mislead you. I just... I've been damn confused ever since my dad's stroke."

"You don't have to do this now, Blake."

"Yeah, I do. Since selling the ranch I've felt...displaced. I didn't know where I was going. Or what I was doing. Or if what I'd done for the last fifteen years of my life was pointless in preparing me for what comes next." He smiled tentatively. "Then I met you. I was totally unprepared for you, sunshine."

Willow didn't say a word.

"These last four days have been amazing."

"For me too."

"You know I've gotta ask...why? I know why they were unforgettable for me, but why for you? Especially when yesterday afternoon you accused me of lying to you."

"I was mad. But I shouldn't have said that... I...I'm sorry."

"Was what happened between us amazing for you only because the sex is so incredible?"

"I'll admit that's part of it. I've never...clicked with anyone the way I have with you."

"Yeah?"

"Yeah. I liked working with you in the bar. I liked talking to you. You make me laugh. You make me feel like I *am* a sexy beauty queen. You make me hot." She smiled. "You make me dinner."

Blake laughed softly.

"You make me feel all those things plus a whole lot more. After I took off and calmed down, I realized I didn't want..."

His hopes sank. "Didn't want what? Me?"

"No!" Willow inhaled a deep breath. "I didn't want you to leave. I want more than four days to get to know everything about you, Blake West."

"Thank God." He reached for her hand and squeezed it. "Does that mean you're okay with me sticking around Broward and tending bar part-time at Dave's until I figure some things out?"

Her shocked expression was priceless. "Really?"

"Yeah. Think maybe you could help me find a place around

here to rent?"

"You could live with me."

Blake shook his head. "I appreciate the offer. But I wanna do this right, Will. What's started between us is too important to screw up. Seems I've been waiting for a woman like you my whole life."

"You'd better define *woman like you*," she teased.

"A perfectly sweet, perfectly hot, perfectly nice woman." He touched the curve of her jaw. "I'm crazy about you."

"I'm pretty crazy about you too."

The moment floated between as sweetly as a promise.

"So what do we do now?"

"Think your crew could do without you for a couple days? I need to go back to Sundance and get my dog and books and stuff. And I'd like to introduce you to my folks on the way back here."

"You sure you want me to come?" Willow smoothed the hair from his forehead. "Won't you be sad to leave your family and home in Wyoming?"

"But that's the thing. I feel like I'm finally coming home."

"You and that sweet talkin'. I could get used to it."

"I sure hope so, sunshine."

"You know, I've been meaning to ask you... Why do you call me sunshine?" Her brow wrinkled. "I'm not blonde. Or even golden skinned."

He grinned at her. "And your disposition isn't particularly sunny when you have a hangover either, which was why it was tongue in cheek when I first started calling you that. But now..."

"But now what?"

"Now, I call you sunshine because you light up my world."

Tears shimmered in her eyes. "I could definitely get used to having you around, Blake West."

"I have a feeling it's gonna be one long, hot summer."

About the Author

To learn more about Lorelei James, please visit www.loreleijames.com. Send an email to lorelei@loreleijames.com or join her Yahoo! group to join in the fun with other readers as well as Lorelei! http://groups.yahoo.com/group/LoreleiJamesGang

Breinigsville, PA USA
22 March 2010
234650BV00002B/2/P